W9-AXP-176

*THE THREE ALIEN SHIPS SHOWED NO
ALARM WHEN THE SINGLE TERRAN VESSEL
APPEARED ALONGSIDE . . .*

"Meda V'Dan," said Mark.

A moment's pause, then: [I am the Lord and Great Captain,
Fateful Dreaming Man. Take warning. You will be punished
proportionately for whatever value you attempt to cheat us
by.]

"I can't object to that—and I give *you* the same warning."

[Do not be presumptuous. It is for us to judge and you to
be judged.]

Suddenly, two more of Mark's cruisers were flanking the
row of Meda V'Dan ships, then three more.

"Now you can board my first vessel to appear here," said
Mark.

[Let him be received in courtesy, and Fateful Dreaming
Man will board your ship.]

"Oh, we're always courteous to our good friends, the
Meda V'Dan."

The Outposter

The Outposter

GORDON R. DICKSON

TOR

A TOM DOHERTY ASSOCIATES BOOK

This is a work of fiction. All the characters and events portrayed in this book are fictional, and any resemblance to real people or incidents is purely coincidental.

THE OUTPOSTER

Copyright © 1972 by Gordon R. Dickson

All rights reserved, including the right to reproduce this book, or portions thereof in any form.

A Tor Book

First printing, June 1982

Second printing, November 1982

ISBN: 0-523-48580-8
Printed in the United States of America

Distributed by:
PINNACLE BOOKS, INC.
1430 Broadway
New York, NY 10018

The Outposter

CHAPTER ONE

The line of those cast out of paradise was three miles long. It stretched along beside the tall wire fence in the drizzling rain, and the unit driver delivering the newly graduated out-poster to the transport ship had to check blowers and honk several times before the line would part enough opposite the final gate in the fence to let the unit through to the passenger side.

Once through both line and gate he turned and drove on the safe side of the fence up to the passenger boarding stairs. The line closed again where it had opened. The gate relocked itself. None of those who had moved bothered to look after the unit. There was a common numbness to them all. It was as if the dark autumn day under the cloud-thick skies had washed all the colour of life out of them, leaving them as drab and chill as itself.

There were now no tears to be seen among them. They moved like people too stupefied for weeping. Those who were going as partners, either because their numbers had been drawn together or because a wife or husband had volunteered to accompany a lotteried mate, held to each other's hands. But that was all.

There was almost no talking. Nearly everyone in the line, from the eighty-year-old lady with the twisted, arthritic fingers to the big young man in the red and gold half coat with the wide, fashionably padded shoulders, carried something—a small overnight case, a brown paper envelope, or a box gift wrapped with bright paper and coloured ribbon. The big young man in red and gold carried a bottle of sixty-three-year-old cognac, holding it in both hands before him as if he could not make up his mind whether to open it just then or not.

In fact, he could not make up his mind—not so much because the decision was a large one, but because two things were at war with him at once, beneath the dispirited indifference that affected them all. He had refused all drugs, but he had let himself drink heavily the night before, which had been as large an evening as he could make it, seeing it was his last on Earth. Therefore, he was sick and vise-headed with the pain of a hangover, and one part of him wanted to open the bottle of cognac to get at the liquor that would help him feel better.

The other part of him that was in conflict with this, however, had something to do with his name, which was Jarl Rakkal. It was a very well-known name, and during the previous three days of indoctrination some of the other drafted colonists had even come up to him for autographs. They had stopped coming when they began to see that he got no better treatment than themselves. The Rakkals were well known in banking circles on Earth, and he had won his own recognition apart from that as publisher of the most successful parti-fax mag to emerge in ten years. He still did not know how his political connections had failed to keep his number out of the lottery. By name and position he should have been doubly secure. Of course, it could have been the doing of his relatives, who had disliked and been ashamed of him. But that no longer mattered. What did matter, now that it was too late, was that being who he was he should be above needing any kind of artificial solace or anesthesia—even to help a hangover as bad as this one—on this boarding day. He was a winner and should not need comforting, even self-administered comforting.

So, he moved along in the slow line, at moments remembering his hangover and instinctively starting to unscrew the top of the bottle, then remembering who he was and checking the twisting fingers.

Ahead of Jarl Rakkal, some eight people ahead in the line, was what seemed to be a child, a young girl of perhaps eight. But there were no children among the lotteried. Actually, what appeared a small girl was a midget, and unlike Jarl she was not at all wondering how she had ended up in the line. Her wonder was that she had not landed in such a line many years before, since variations from the physical norm were caught in the lottery more often than average people. Her name was Lily Betaugh, and she had set out to be a university teacher of philosophy of such stature that she would be voted exemption from the lottery.

She had in fact become a full professor of philosophy, at the University of Belgrade, but she had never become either popular or famous enough to be voted exemption. Sometime during the last few years she had realized that she never would. She was brilliant—very, very brilliant. But she wasn't the best, and only the best got exemptions.

Some thirty yards farther up the line of drafted colonists—almost level with the unit from which newly graduated Outposter Mark Ten Roos was now alighting, on the far side of the fence—was Age Hammerschold. He was a master cabinetmaker, overage for union protection but by a year and a half still young enough for the lottery, and now his chief mental activity was to congratulate himself continually that his wife had died three years before. The thought filled him with something like glee—it was as if he, personally, had successfully cheated the authorities out of one body and one soul by having had a wife who died before he himself could be drafted. He waited his turn on the boarding ladder leading to the colonists' ship entrance almost with indifference. He was close enough to hear what they were saying on the other side of the high fence with the barbed wire top, but he paid no attention. As far as he was concerned, the regular passengers were like so many exotic animals with which he had nothing in common.

"Miss," the shorter of the ship's guards on the far side of the fence was saying, "you don't understand."

"Oh, I understand," answered the girl passenger he was talking to. She extended a slim right arm and pulled back the cuff on its semitransparent black sleeve. Strapped to her wrist was the small matchbox shape of a wrist gun. "But I've got a weapon."

For the first time, Mark Ten Roos, the young outposter who had just arrived, took a close look at her. She was no older than Mark, tall and slimly athletic, with a shoulder-length mane of black hair bound with a silver band that held it back from the delicate oval of her face. Her eyes sparkled now, just on the edge of an explosion of anger, and the little wrist gun had a pattern of red and green jewels set in its case.

"Yes, miss," said one of the two guards, "I know. But that's not the point. Ship's regulation is for all passengers to wear *side arms*"— he held up the ship-issued belt and weapon he had been offering her, as if she were a judge before whom he was presenting evidence. "It's captain's regulations, miss."

It was curious, Mark thought, that the guards were being so unusually patient with the girl. He wondered who she was. No salesman's wife would have received such kidglove treatment, and in any case she looked

too young to be one of the embarking wives.
But even a member of the staff of an admiral-
general, like the one named on the ship's
transport schedule Mark had examined
earlier, was hardly likely to rate such patient
handling.

Clearly she could not be as mere a person as
a salesman's wife or even a high-ranking staff
member. She could only be, like the admiral-
general himself, a member of the so-called
Five Thousand—that rarefied social aristocracy of an overpopulated Earth, among
whom unlimited wealth and unlimited power
were taken for granted; that select community so isolated from the rest of the people of
the Earth-City and the Colonies that the aristocrats even effected a private slang of their
own, with fashionable pet names for one
another which changed with every season.

Mark stared at this girl now. In spite of himself, she attracted him, like some pure jewel
in an ostentatious setting of great richness
and craft. Everything about her was the
symbol of all he had spent his knowledgeable
years in detesting—but, she herself was beautiful. Beautiful and young, and so wrapped in
luxury that she could not conceive of its lack.
To her, a jaunt to the Colonies would be a
play-trip, an adventure . . .

He put her coldly from his mind and turned
back to his examination of the colonists and
the spaceship.

She was a one-hundred-and-fifty-thousand-
ton vessel, the *Wombat*, ready for takeoff to
the Abruzzi Sector of colonized space—that

sector protected by Outer Space Navy Base One, where nine-tenths of the colonized worlds were to be found, circling half a dozen closely related stars. Takeoff was scheduled for two hours from now. Right at the moment, the *Wombat* lay on her belly in her berth on Spaceport, South Pacific, a great floating pad of concrete five hundred miles due north from the Marquesas.

Her cargo, according to the transport schedule, was machine tools, instruments, weapons, and some twelve hundred colonists destined for assignment to colonies on the four colonized worlds under the sun of Garnera, a GO-type star with a family of eighteen planets. Her passengers included the admiral-general of Space Navy Force Blue One at the Outer Navy Base, with his personal party of six, and twenty-three manufacturers' representatives or salesmen, four with wives. Also, three outposters including Mark himself.

Mark caught sight of his reflection in the tall silver case of a plasma power generator awaiting loading. The figure that looked back at him was that of a tall, lean, rather long-faced youth, with dark and penetrating eyes, in the utilitarian boots, jump suit, and short jacket of an experienced outposter. A side arm rested openly in a topless grey holster fitted flat to the belt around his narrow waist and clamped to the grey cloth of the pants' leg over the outside of his right thigh. Clamped likewise around the grey-sleeved biceps of his left arm was the black metal band and seal that proclaimed his outposter rank. If it had not been for the youthfulness of his features, there would have been no reason for the slightly startled look on the face of the guard at the outer gate of the spaceport's closed field area, several minutes ago.

At the memory of that look, a cool breath of humour blew for a second across Mark's mind. It would not be a usual sight for the guard—the face of someone as young as Mark and wearing gun and grey, like a veteran of the Outpost Stations. Even newly graduated outposters like himself, Mark knew, were normally three to five years older than he was.

His attention was drawn back to the long line of figures some twenty yards away, beyond the wire fence, streaming slowly aboard the ship through a cargo hatch. Men and women alike, they moved without protest. But their faces were sombre, and not a few of them were pale with inner fear or a hangover. Only here and there was a zombie-like figure helped along by a friend or a wife, having been put under heavy tranquillization for his own emotional relief, or because he had caused trouble in the staging area.

At this moment they looked like an ordinary batch—a simple cross section of humanity from the Earth-City. But in their present stage of shock it was impossible to tell. Right now their minds were full only of the fact that they were being sent out. Later, when the shock wore off, it would be possible for the outposters aboard to weigh and judge them, to read their characters and take advantage of being on shipboard with them to put in priority claims for the more likely ones.

Mark continued to watch them come, now,
for his own reasons. Whether by accident or
design, most of them had chosen to dress
themselves in colours as sombre as their
faces. Only far down the line approaching the
ship was there one flash of brilliant colour—
a big man dressed in a half-coat of scarlet and
gold, with calf-high boots of dark blue and a
golden cap.

The argument at the foot of the passenger
stairs, just in front of him, drew Mark's attention once more from the colonists.

"I don't see why!" The girl was angry now.
"My gun is just as lethal at short range as
that."

"But part of the point is in showing the
weapon, miss," said the guard she was facing.
"It's part of the necessary early conditioning
for the gar—the colonists."

"The what?" The girl stared at him.

The guard's face reddened. The word had
almost slipped out, and any explanation now
would simply make matters worse. Mark
examined the guard with new interest to see
how he would handle the situation.

"The—colonists, miss," he stammered.
"You see—"

"But you started to call them 'garbage'!" ex-
claimed the girl, staring at him. "That's a ter-
rible thing to say!"

"Well, it's not them, so much—" the guard
was now sweating lightly. "We—they just call
them that because the Earth-City's got to get
rid of . . . well, what it doesn't want . . ."

The other guard, Mark noted, was prudent-
ly staying out of it. From social error his
partner was now sinking into near treason,
and this before someone who, by evidence of
the unusual respect they had shown her,
might well be closely related to someone in
the Earth-City government. Mark felt a twinge
of sympathy for the guard. Rescue should not
be too difficult. What was needed was a diver-
sion.

He glanced back at the approaching line of
colonists. The big man in the scarlet and gold
clothing was now almost opposite them. It
was obvious that his wearing apparel, when
seen up close, was every bit as expensive as
that of the girl's, but wealth alone was not
always enough to keep someone from being
lotteried for the colonies. The colonist's
heavy-boned, good-looking face had a wild,
pale look, and there was the glint of sweat on
his broad forehead. Mark guessed him to be
suffering not only from being where he was
but also from a drug or alcohol hangover.
Mark stared at the man hard, and after a
second, with the sensitivity of the watched,
the big man looked around. Through the wire
mesh of the ten-foot-high fence their eyes met.

Mark smiled at him, deliberately—with the
mocking smile of someone on the right side of
the barrier.

For a second Jarl Rakkal only stared back.
Then his face spasmed into a white mask. And
suddenly he was running toward the fence.

Shouts from the other colonists interrupted
the girl and the now-babbling guard. Both

guards swung about as the big man went up the far side of the fence like a cat, his hands clamping fiercely on the wire ends at the top and coming away bloody as he flipped his body over and down on the passenger side.

The guard who had not been in trouble had his gun half drawn. Mark reached over and knocked it back down into the holster.

"I'll handle it," Mark said.

He turned and took three steps to meet the charging colonist. Some six feet from him, the scarlet and gold figure suddenly bent double without breaking stride and launched itself like a missile—right arm stiffly outstretched, hand open, and fingers up, the butt of the palm leading at an almost impossible angle with the wrist.

It was a *ki* stroke, by one who was more than a casual amateur in that school of unarmed combat. The advantage of momentum and angle was all with the attacker, as the staring guards, if not the girl, knew. The counter was as simple as the *ki* stroke itself, but like the *ki* stroke, its success depended upon that sort of split-second timing acquired only by monotonous and countless hours of practice.

In the fraction of a second before the lethal palm-butt touched him, Mark fell stiffly off to his left side, catching himself on his outstretched left arm and levering his right leg up and out stiffly in a sideways kick. The rising bar of his leg slammed into the groin of his flying attacker and flipped the body in midair, landing it heavily on its back a few yards beyond. The big man, stunned, tried momentarily to rise, then fell back unconscious.

The guards were upon him immediately, pinning the unresisting arms and legs. One of them produced a hypo gun loaded with a tranquillizer; the other spoke rapidly into the phone on his wrist and called for extra guards. Mark walked over to them as they finished their several tasks.

"What's his number?" Mark asked. "I may want him."

The guard who had just finished using his phone reached for the tag around the tanned throat of the unconscious colonist.

"Sixteen hundred and twenty-nine, of yesterday's date," the guard said.

"Thanks," said Mark.

"Not at all, sir." The guard who had answered was the one who had been talking himself into trouble with the girl. He looked at Mark now with gratitude mingled with a new respect that ignored Mark's youthfulness. "That was pretty, that counter."

"Thanks," said Mark. He turned and went back over to where the girl was standing, staring down at the fallen man. For a moment, seeing the look on her face, he felt something almost like a surge of sympathy for her.

"You see," he told her, "a pellet from a little wrist gun like yours won't stop a charge like that. But a heavy slug from a side arm will. It has more mass, and so more stopping power."

Her head came around slowly. She stared at him incredulously for a second. Then, instinctively, he took a step backward and the open edge of her hand lashed past his face.

"You—" she choked it off. "Did you have to hurt him like that? You—disposable!"

She turned and ran to kneel by the still-unconscious figure. Left standing, Mark smiled a little grimly. Her class instinct had not been slow in reasserting itself.

"Take him into my cabin!" she ordered the guards, busy on both sides of her.

"I'm sorry, miss—" began the guard who had argued with her about wearing the side arm.

"Did you hear me? I said take him into my cabin! Don't you know who he is? He's Jarl Rakkal!"

Official patience finally gave out.

"I wouldn't care if he was your father himself!" snapped the guard. "Who he is doesn't mean anything here. I know what he is, and that's a colonist. He goes back on the other side of the fence and lucky that's all that'll happen to him. Now, get out of our way. And put that side arm on before you try to enter the ship!"

The guard turned his back on her and spoke to his mate.

"Lift, Harry."

Together, they picked up the limp body of Jarl Rakkal between them and carried it toward the little gate in the fence between the two landing stairs. The girl was left on her knees, staring after them. For a moment Mark hesitated, gazing at her. Then he turned away and mounted the passenger stairs.

He stepped into the entry lounge and paused there at the desk of the duty officer to show his papers and give his name. The officer accepted them with one hand, meanwhile looking past Mark to the scene down by the foot of the stairs.

"Admiral-General Jas Showell's kid," he said looking back at Mark. "Daddy should explain a few things to her." He glanced at Mark's papers, then at Mark's face. *"Destination Garnera Six, Abruzzi Fourteen Station. First tour as an outposter?"*

"That's right. But I was born out there," said Mark.

"Oh," said the duty officer. He stamped Mark's papers with the ship's signet and passed them back to him. "You'll be in stateroom K Fourteen. Oh, by the way, here's a message that just came for you. To be held for your arrival on board."

"Thanks," said Mark.

He took the small, grey tube of the message cartridge and went past the desk, turning left down the long corridor gleaming whitely with the plastic surfacing that in this forward part of the ship hid the bare metal work of its structure. He passed the first circular ladder he came to, but mounted the second. At the first level up, he paused to sniff at a strange, flat scentlessness of the air. Then he continued up one more level to a narrower, carpeted corridor along which he found the numbered door of his stateroom.

He touched the blue latch button in the white concave outer surface of the door and

stepped through as the door slid aside. It shut
noiselessly behind him, and he looked about
the twenty-by-seven-foot cubicle typical of a
first-class accommodation on a ship like this.
Two inflated armchairs, a table, and a short
couch had already been extruded from panels
in the walls, ready for his waking-hours occu-
pancy. Other panels, still closed, held the
collapsed structures that would transform
the day-lounge appearance of the compartment into a bedroom for sleeping. He made a
routine examination of the room, its equipment and storage cabinets, before taking out
a message player and extruding a side table
by one of the armchairs to hold it.

He sat down in the armchair, inserted the
message into the player, and flicked the
switch.

Abruptly the appearance of the compartment was gone from around him. Instead, he
appeared to be seated in a room he knew well
—the library-study of Wilkes Danielson,
Mark's tutor since Mark's arrival on Earth
from Garnera VI, five years before. The
library was unchanged except for a new
bookcase filling the corner where Mark's
study console had formerly sat, to the left of
the tall window on the other side of which was
Wilkes's own console. Otherwise, in its heavy
reference files, its bookcases full of ancient,
paper-sheeted, cardboard-and-leather-bound
books, the old room was the same.

Mark could almost smell the books. Wilkes
was sitting in his high wing chair, swivelled
around now, away from his console, as Mark

had seen him sit so many times in the evenings when their study periods were over, and their talk went off into many other topics—those same talks which had grown scarce, these last few years, as Mark had become more and more involved in the training needed to qualify him for his certificate as an outposter.

Now the image of Wilkes Danielson looked at him—a slight, thin, black man in his mid-fifties, almost bald, but with something fragilely handsome and still youthful about him, underneath the wrinkles and the near-vanished hairline. The lips of the image moved, and Wilkes's voice came to Mark's ears.

"Hello, Mark," it said. "I deliberately sent this on ahead of the ship, so that you wouldn't think I was still trying to talk you out of going."

Wilkes hesitated.

"I've done something you probably won't approve of—I don't know," he went on. "You never told me exactly why you wanted to go out and lose yourself there among the Colonies, when what everyone else wants—a secure home here in the Earth-City—could be yours almost for the asking. There are only ten Trophy winners in any academic year. With your Trophy and my recommendation it'd be only a matter of time until you made enough of a success for yourself, in any one of half a dozen fields, to be voted permanent exemption from the lottery . . . but we've gone into this before . . ."

Wilkes's eyes wandered. Once more he seemed to search for words.

"I've never challenged you about your going out," he went on, after a few seconds, "because I knew there was no point in asking if you didn't want to tell me. Ever since your foster father first sent you to me—a thirteen-year-old fresh from the Outposts—I've known two things. One, your mind isn't going to be changed on anything you set out to do, and two, whatever it is, if it's humanly possible, you'll end up doing it."

He hesitated.

"You're too intelligent to dedicate yourself to getting revenge for your parents—even if revenge were possible. How could anyone ever track down a Meda V'Dan ship that burned an Outpost eighteen years ago? But what bothers all of us who've known you here is what other reason could there be for burying yourself in the Outposts and Colonies? You're something more than just a Trophy winner, Mark. I've tutored Trophy winners before, which is why I've got my own exemption from the lottery. But in twenty-four years, Mark, I've never turned out one like you—"

The thin, little man made a nervous gesture with one hand and dropped the subject in mid-sentence.

"Never mind that," he said. "You'll be wondering when I'll get to the point, and what the point is. Briefly, it's that I've gone ahead and recommended you for the anthropology post at Alamogordo, just as if you were staying here on Earth. And when they start to

process it and find you gone, I'll continue re-
newing my recommendation as long as I live."

He straightened up and looked more directly into the recorder that had taken down the
message.

"Which won't be long," he said. "I've had a
new assessment of my bone cancer. A year
and a half, they say now, at the most. After
that, you'll always be able to come home to
the Earth-City like any other outposter, but
your chances of starting a career that can lead
to lottery exemption are going to be close to
zero. In a year and a half there will be two
new classes of Trophy winners, and their
tutors will still be alive and pushing them for
all the posts that count.

"Think about it, Mark, during the next year
and a half," Wilkes said. "The Earth-City
needs you, and you need it."

The message ended abruptly, and the stateroom was again visible around Mark. He
reached out and took the message unit from
the player, opened a wall compartment, and
put both message and player out of sight.

He had been close to Wilkes, as close as he
had been to anyone on Earth. With an effort of
will, he shrugged off the emotional appeal of
the older man's message and put both of them
out of his mind at once.

Curiously, disconcertingly, he found himself thinking instead about the girl at the
foot of the boarding stairs, and loneliness was
like a chill, heavy hand pressing down upon
him.

CHAPTER TWO

At 0643 hours, local time, loading was completed, all outer and inner doors locked, and the *Wombat* lifted. Four hours later the ship broke traffic pattern from Earth orbit and headed for open space on plasma engines. Nineteen hours after that, all doors still locked and personnel in position, it went into preparation for the first transportation shift.

Twenty minutes later, with the shift successfully completed and recalculation begun, the sound of three notes chimed throughout the ship, including the speaker panel in one wall of Mark's stateroom.

"The ship is now interstellar," said a voice from the panel as the last note died away. "All normal doors on unlock. The passenger lounge and dining areas are now open for service."

Mark, who had waked from a light doze with the sound of the chimes, rose, and shaved and dressed as carefully as if he were still a trainee and going on parade. He checked his side arm, slipped it into its leg holster, and went out of his room toward the main dining lounge.

When he got there, the tables scattered around the wide, low-ceilinged but pleasant room were empty, except for one to the right of the door, halfway between it and a long table set against a farther wall. It was a small table set for three, and two men in outposter grey were already occupying two of its chairs, facing each other.

One was a man no more than in his mid-thirties but already half-bald, his close-cropped black hair like a tonsure above his narrow, tanned face. The other man was perhaps ten years older, tall and built like an athlete, with stubbled grey-blond hair fitting his round head like a cap. The black-haired man was eating a steak, while the other was involved with a large order of ham and eggs. There was a bottle of aquavit in a bowl of ice on the table between them, already down by perhaps a sixth of its contents. Both men's side arms were drawn and laid on the table to the right of their plates.

Mark, nodding to the half-bowing dining-room steward, walked over to the empty chair at their table and stood behind it.

The other two went on eating and drinking without looking up. After a little more than a minute the black-haired man raised his eyes from his plate, but only to look across the table at the outposter opposite.

"Looks like we've got ourselves another apprentice, Whin," he said.

"I noticed," said Whin. His voice was more tenor than baritone, and slightly hoarse. He poured himself a small shot of the colourless, powerful liquor and swallowed it. Then, still without looking up, he added, "What's your name, Prents?"

"Mark William Ten Roos," said Mark. "For Abruzzi Fourteen Station, Garnera Six."

"That's Brot Halliday's station," said the black-haired man. For the first time, he glanced up at Mark and examined him briefly, before turning back to Whin. "This must be that kid who's a Trophy winner. Chav and Lila's boy—you remember, Whin? Brot adopted him after a Meda V'Dan ship hit their Post Station, seventeen years ago—that right, Prents?"

"Eighteen," said Mark.

"Second generation," said Whin with his mouth full. He swallowed and he too glanced up at Mark. "Doesn't look much different from any other Prents to me. Want to let him sit down?"

"Don't mind if you don't," said the other. He looked at Mark. "Sit down, Prents."

Mark drew his side arm, laid it to the right of the plate on the table before him, and sat down. He did not touch the menu on the plate or anything on the table.

"Know who you're talking to, Prents?" asked the dark-haired man. Mark nodded. "I checked the passenger and cargo lists before boarding," he said. "Senior Outposter Alvin Morthar and"—he looked at Whin—"Outpost Station Master Whinfeld Orby Proith."

"All right," said Whin. "Let him eat, Al?"

"Why not? Go ahead and order, Prents."

Mark picked up the menu and unfolded it. To the understeward who materialized at his elbow, he indicated the second line from the bottom of the left-hand page.

"Number four," he said. "Bacon, eggs, coffee."

"Coffee?" said Alvin Morthar. He reached for the aquavit bottle and poured half a water-glassful into a tumbler before Mark's plate. "Drink that, Prents."

"Thanks," said Mark, without moving to pick up the glass. "But no, thank you."

"No!" Al's black eyebrows were suddenly straight in line above his eyes. He was not smiling. "Did you say no to me, Prents?"

"Sorry," said Mark, looking back at him. "I may have duties."

"Duties?" It was Whin. "What duties? You're not on Post yet."

"There's a Meda V'Dan aboard," said Mark.

The two old outposters stared at him.

"What're you talking about, Ten Roos?" said Al. "There wasn't any Meda V'Dan on the passenger list I saw."

"Probably he's one of the party of six listed with Admiral-General Jaseth Showell," said Mark.

The other two sat looking hard at him.

"You've got something special against the aliens on account of your folks, is that it?" Whin said.

"Yes," said Mark.

"What've you got in mind for this one—if

there is one?" said Al. "Come to think of it, if the alien's not listed, how do you know he's aboard?"

"They have deodorizers working on level *J* —didn't you smell the difference in the air there when you came aboard?" Mark said. "There's no reason for deodorizers in the passenger section unless it's to make it possible for a Meda V'Dan to live with us."

Whin nodded, rubbing his lower lip thoughtfully with a long, heavy forefinger. "Sounds like it," he said.

"I asked you," said Al, "what you had in mind for this alien if he is aboard."

"I just want to send a message with him to the other Meda V'Dan," said Mark.

"What kind of message?"

"That Abruzzi Fourteen Station is open for trading."

Al turned to Whin. "The kid wants to be raided," Al said, "so he can kill him some aliens."

"Just so long as he doesn't plan to kill one on board here," said Whin. He turned pale, flat-looking blue eyes on Mark. "You aren't planning to use your gun on this Meda V'Dan?"

"Only in self-defence."

"Then there's no worry," said Whin to Al. "Whoever the alien is, he won't even talk to anyone but his own interpreter, let alone admit he recognizes an outposter in the same room with him."

"Good enough," said Al, sitting back. He turned to Mark. "But I think, just to play safe, you better drink down that aquavit after all."

Mark did not move to pick up the glass.

"Duties," he said.

Their eyes locked.

"Let's not push him, Al," said Whin unexpectedly. "'Duties' is a big word."

Al sat back again.

"All right, Prents," he said. "But you better look good every way else the rest of this trip."

The understeward came with Mark's breakfast order, but as he picked up a fork to eat, a female voice spoke at his ear.

"Sir—Mr. Ten Roos? If you don't mind?"

He turned, saw the girl of the landing stairs, and got to his feet, pushing his chair back.

"Miss Showell?" he said. "Have you met Senior Outposter Alvin Morthar, Outpost Station Master Whinfeld Orby Proith?"

"Oh, pleased to meet you both." She looked at Mark. "But could I speak to you privately for a moment, though?"

"Of course." Mark followed her toward the empty side of the room where the long table gleaming with silverware still waited for the ship's captain and his particular guests.

"I'm sorry," she said, in a low voice, halting at last beside the long table. "I wanted to apologize for acting the way I did out there. The guards explained to me that they'd have had to shoot Jarl if you hadn't stopped him the way you did. You really saved his life for him, doing what you did. I didn't understand."

Her tone was soft, almost humble. They were standing close together, and she was dressed now in some flowing, filmy blue stuff that floated around her as she moved and hovered as she stayed still. Within it, looking down at the floor, she seemed both small and innocent, and once more he felt the deep attraction to her that had laid hold of him when he had first seen her outside the ship. He had to remind himself that all that operated upon his emotion was probably a pose, that she was of that class accustomed to getting its own way regardless of the means used.

She would, Mark told himself, have something up her sleeve, to seek him out and apologize this way. However forewarned was forearmed, and it would do no harm to play along with her until her motives were revealed.

"I didn't expect you to," said Mark.

"But that's no excuse. I should have known." She smiled up at him. "But it's like someone like you, I suppose, not to blame me. Look, I'd like my father to meet someone like you. He's—oh, I suppose you know?"

"Admiral-General Showell." Mark nodded.

"Why don't you have breakfast with us here, at the captain's table?"

"Thank you," said Mark, "but the captain hasn't asked me. Also, I've already ordered breakfast at my regular table."

"They can bring it over here. And don't worry about the captain. As long as you're part of Dad's party—" She broke off to turn and speak to a passing understeward about bringing Mark's breakfast order to the captain's table.

"Come on," she said, leading him up the

table to two chairs near the head of it, "sit down with me here, and tell me about outposters. It's really sad. I don't know anything about your people. I don't think Dad does either—the way he should."

She pulled a chair out from the table. He held it for her as she sat down, then took the chair beside it that she had pointed out a second before.

"Would you like a drink?" she said, as an understeward came to hover over them. "No? I'll have a crushed rum and orange juice, steward. Mark—you don't mind my calling you Mark?" There was a glittering cube of some polished material hanging by a chain around her neck—an expensive alien ornament of the sort in which the Meda V'Dan traded. It twirled, catching his eyes with flashes of light as she spoke.

"No," said Mark.

"I asked the duty officer your name when I came on board. My name's Ulla. You can call me that if you like." She grimaced. "That was pretty bad of me out there. I called you a "disposable." That's as bad as calling the colonists "garbage.""

An understeward slid a tall fluted glass of orange liquid before Ulla and placed a plate with bacon and eggs in front of Mark.

"The names exist," said Mark. "And everyone's got one."

"Everyone?" She stared at him, her glass in hand. "Oh, go ahead and eat. But there are only you outposters and the colonists out there who have names."

"There's the Navy. And the Meda V'Dan."

The pupils of her eyes enlarged.

"The Navy?" she echoed. "You mean the men under Dad's command at some place like Blue One—there's a name for *them?*"

"Men and officers. Everyone," said Mark, eating. "They're called 'scarecrows.'"

"Scarecrows?" She had put her glass back down without tasting its contents. "Why?"

"Because they're supposed to keep the rats away from the garbage, just by being there—and being there is all they do," Mark said. An understeward put down a cup of coffee by his plate, and he stopped eating to drink. Putting the cup back down he looked directly at Ulla.

"Rats?" she asked.

"It's as good a name as any," he said, "for the Meda V'dan." He went back to eating his breakfast.

"But the aliens don't do anything but trade nowadays," she said. "They don't dare with the Navy there. Oh, I understand they're different from us and one of them goes renegade once in a long while—"

"No," he said.

"No?" She stared at him until he stopped eating once more to look at her.

"The Meda V'Dan only trade when they have to," Mark said. "Otherwise they raid the Outposts for supplies. When the supplies don't get replaced in time, people die."

He was looking directly at her. She stared back at him with a fixed gaze.

"*Die?*" she echoed. "The . . . poor colonists."

"No," he said. "It's the poor outposters. They're the ones who get killed when their stations are raided. If their colonists have training, guts, and energy, they can scratch out a living until fresh supplies come."

She shook her head slowly, watching him.

"It isn't what you say," she commented slowly. "It's the tone of your voice when you say it. I never heard anyone sound so bitter. Besides, everybody knows the Navy protects the stations."

"The Navy—" he began, but the sound of voices from the entrance to the dining lounge interrupted. They both turned to look.

Entering the dining room and coming toward the head of the long table were a small, spare, sharp-eyed, middle-aged man in civilian clothes, a tall heavy man of roughly the same age in captain's uniform, a tall younger man also in civilian clothes, and another individual. This fourth one wore soft, loose clothing—a multicoloured, striped shirt-like upper garment with billowing sleeves and loose checkered pants. The shirt sleeves were cuffed tight to the narrow wrists of long greyish-white hands; a broad belt held two knives and a side arm with a twisted, jewelled butt; the pants were stuffed into red boots that would have been calf high on a man. Above all this colour the unnaturally narrow face of the Meda V'Dan was strangely drab and placid with its grey-white skin. Only two patches of black hair on the lower cheeks caught the eye, in contrast to the long, narrow, shaven skull. Bringing up the rear were two of the ship's crewmen in dress guard uniforms, wearing side arms and carrying plasma rifles.

"There you are, Ulla!" called the sharp-eyed spare little man, who was leading the group. "No, no, don't get up, you and your friend. We'll all be sitting in a moment."

The group reached the long table and sorted itself out. The captain took the head of the table with the small man at his right, in the chair on the other side of Ulla. The Meda V'Dan was ushered to the chair on the captain's left, opposite the small man, with the younger man in civilian clothes at the left of the alien.

"Daddy," said Ulla to the small man, "this is Outposter Mark Ten Roos—"

But Mark was already getting to his feet, knife and fork still in his hand.

"I'm sorry," he said to the table, looking around at all of them, but bringing his eyes at last to bear on the Meda V'Dan, who looked back—not directly, but at a point just past Mark's right shoulder—"the Abruzzi Fourteen Station is always open to the Meda V'Dan for trade. But I trade with them, I don't eat with them."

He laid his fork and knife back down on the plate, the two utensils crossed, the edge of the knife toward the alien.

With an explosive sound from his throat, the Meda V'Dan was suddenly on his feet, the civilian beside him also rising hastily.

"What's this? What is this?" snapped the small man, looking from Mark to the alien.

"Admiral," said the younger man beside the Meda V'Dan, "he's been insulted."

"Insulted? What do you mean insulted?" Admiral-General Showell stared at Mark, who did not answer, then switched his gaze back to the younger man across the table. "Insulted how?"

"I don't know, sir." The younger man's face was pale.

"You're the interpreter! Ask him!"

The interpreter turned to the Meda V'Dan and spoke for a few moments in a heavy, coughing series of sounds. The Meda V'Dan, still facing Mark and staring past Mark's shoulder, answered in a rapid rolling of similar sounds.

"The Lord and Great Captain"—the interpreter interrupted himself with a series of throaty, explosive sounds that came out sounding something like *Hov'rah Min Hlan*— "whose name means Sleepless Under Oath in our primitive tongue, has been offended by an intimation that he is . . ." the interpreter hesitated momentarily, glancing at Ulla, "a gelded male who hides behind females."

The interpreter pointed to the crossed knife and fork.

"You see, Admiral," he said, "the knife is under the fork—"

"Guards!" It was the captain at the head of the table, on his feet also now, his heavy-fleshed face flushed. "Put that outposter under arrest!"

Mark took one step back from the table so that he had the guards and the Meda V'Dan all in view at once. His right hand lifted a little so that it was above the butt of his side arm. The two guards hesitated. They were men hardly older than Mark, who had plainly never fired a weapon in anger nor had they expected to do so.

"What're you waiting for?" snapped the captain. "I said arrest him! If he gives you any trouble—"

"All right! Hold it. Hold it!" broke in the hoarse, tenor voice of Whin, and a second later his tall, wide-shouldered figure stepped in between Mark and the two armed guards— much to the guards' plain relief.

"If he gives you any trouble," Whin said to the captain, "I'll deal with him myself. But your tin sheep aren't shooting any outposters, now or ever. And you aren't putting any under arrest, either, for the sake of a skunk of a Meda V'Dan."

CHAPTER THREE

For a short, breathless second, no one else
spoke or moved. Then the dry sound of
Admiral-General Showell's laughing broke
the tension.

"Well, Captain?" Showell said. "Are you
going to arrest them both, then? Or all three
of them?"

"Sir!" said the captain, his face flooded
with colour, almost glaring down at his
superior officer.

"Give it up, Juan. Give it up," replied
Showell. "We don't arrest outposters away
from Earth, and they don't arrest Navy men.
We need each other out on the Colonies. Call
your guards off."

"Ground arms," said the captain sulkily to
the two guards, who dropped the plasma
rifles quickly, butt down on the carpet, upper
barrels held at their trousered sides.

"But," said the still-seated Showell, turning
to look up at Whin, "I'll leave it up to you to
calm down the—er—Lord and Great Captain,

who is our guest."

"He's already calmed down." Whin looked across at Sleepless Under Oath, who transferred his gaze to a point just past the right shoulder of the older outposter. "Hov'rah Min Hlan, a ship of your people—"

The interpreter hastily began to translate.

"Shut up," said Whin. "He understands me just as well as I understand him when he speaks his own tongue, and a lot better than he follows that hash you make of trying to talk a language you haven't got the jaws or vocal cords to handle. As I was saying, Hov'rah Min Hlan, a ship of the Meda V'Dan killed this boy's parents six weeks after he was born, at Abruzzi Fifteen Station. He holds your whole people under blood guilt to him. He can do or say anything he wants to you individually, without involving any other men or Meda V'Dan."

Without changing the off-angle of his fixed gaze, Sleepless Under Oath rattled off a throaty string of sounds.

"Sure," said Whin. "Oh, sure, we understand that. They were renegades, and the Meda V'Dan will punish them if found."

He turned to Mark.

"What do you say about that, Ten Roos?" the big outposter demanded. "Or didn't *you* understand him?"

"I understood him perfectly," said Mark. "And my answer is that the day the renegades are punished before me, I'll absolve the rest of the Meda V'Dan of blood guilt. Until then, any one of them I meet may be one of those who destroyed the Abruzzi Fifteen Station."

Sleepless Under Oath said a few short syllables and sat down, transferring his gaze to the table before him.

"All right. I don't see him either—for the rest of this trip," said Mark.

He turned and walked out of the dining lounge. A few steps away down the corridor outside, he heard the voice of Whin behind him.

"Hold it."

Mark stopped and turned to face the larger, older man.

"Just a minute, Ten Roos," said Whin. "I told them in there that none of them was going to shoot an outposter, but it could be *I* might. What makes you think you can play games with Meda V'Dan on a Navy ship just to make yourself feel good without counting the consequences?"

"I counted the consequences," said Mark.

"You mean you counted on Al and me to get you out of any trouble you got yourself in?" The lines on Whin's tanned brow deepened into hard ridges.

"I expected you to help," said Mark. "But I was ready to get myself out if I had to."

"Get yourself out!" Whin stared at him. "You think you can take on a whole ship, even of Navy men, with one side arm?"

"Not exactly—"

"No, not exactly!" snorted Whin. "Anyway, that's not what matters. The point you've got to learn is that the principle of every outposter backing up every other outposter

wasn't invented just so you could stick pins in any Meda V'Dan you meet and get away without being hurt. It's a law we came up with, and proved with the blood of some good men, so that we could at least live with a Navy that has no more guts and principle out among the stars than a fat rabbit. And you're going to learn what the law means. I'm restricting you to your cabin for the rest of the trip, and when you get to Brot Halliday, you'll bring him a message from me telling him to finish your education about matters like this."

"No," said Mark quietly. "I'm not accepting any restriction, and I'll carry no message."

Whin took a half step back from him, so they were now far enough apart to have a full vision of each other from boot caps to skull top. The big man's right hand lifted above his holster, which once more held the gun that had lain beside his plate on the table.

"Boy," said Whin gently, "maybe being a Trophy winner back at the Earth-City's gone to your head. Maybe you think reflexes and marksmanship are all there is to it. You want to fight *me?*"

"Not unless I have to," said Mark. "But I can't stay shut up in my stateroom this trip, or anything else. I've got duties."

"Getting revenge for your folks," said Whin still softly, "that's something to do in your spare time, and without involving other outposters."

"Not just that," said Mark. "I've got a bigger job to do. How would you like the

Colonies and Outposts with no more Meda V'Dan?"

Whin stared at him.

"No more . . ." His voice trailed off. "You had your psychological tests before you were passed?"

"Yes," said Mark. "I rated AA One."

"And you're not out to get just one Lord and Great Captain with his shipload of pirates, you're after them all?" Whin shook his head. "Those tests missed for once."

"Maybe," said Mark. "Maybe not. Worth your finding out?"

Whin's spread hand sank slowly to his side, until his thumb touched, relaxed, against the side of his holster.

"You're a strange one," he said, staring at Mark. After a second, he shook his head. "But you're second generation, and maybe that means something."

"Maybe," said Mark.

Whin took a deep breath.

"All right," he said. "How do you plan to clean out a whole race of aliens?"

"I'm sorry," said Mark. "If it was the kind of thing I could explain to people, I'd have talked about it before now. This is something I'm going to have to work on alone."

Whin's eyes squeezed themselves narrow between the wrinkled lids and the wrinkled sun creases of the skin below.

"I'm just supposed to take your word for it, then?" he said.

"My word, and the fact I won't confine myself on this trip under anyone's orders," said

Mark. "It meant enough to me that I'm willing to back my freedom up right now if I have to. And, just as you said, I know there's more to a gunfight than just good reflexes and marksmanship."

"Yes," said Whin. He stood looming over Mark, staring down at him for a long moment. Then he turned and walked away.

"Mark?"

It was a hesitant question from Ulla Showell behind him. Mark turned to see her standing a few feet away, just to the right of the entrance to the dining room. He waited and she came up to him, looking at him as if seeing him from some new, strange angle.

"Forgive me," he said, "for interrupting your breakfast."

"There's nothing to forgive," she said. She was a little pale. She glanced back at the dining room entrance and then up at him. "Let's walk a little way away from here, why don't we?"

He nodded. Together they turned and moved off down the empty, cleanly carpeted corridor.

"I didn't have any idea," she said, after they had gone some little way without saying anything, "you felt that way about the Meda V'Dan. I thought you were just someone who'd picked the outposts as a career, or to stay out of government service during your draft years."

"No," he smiled a little. "I'm what they call in the Outposts a second-generation man. The children of outposters usually get sent to

Earth to finish their education, but most of them don't stay there. They come back to the Outposts again."

"Even when they know what it's like?" she asked. "Even when they've seen people in their own family killed, like you?"

He smiled again.

"I may have seen it," he said, "but I don't remember it. I was only six weeks old. All I know is what the outposters from Brot Halliday's station—he's been my foster father since—told me when I got a little older."

She shook her head, looking sideways and up at him as they walked together. Her eyes were large and dark; and, happening to meet them for a second as he glanced down at her, he found her once more strangely disturbing to his mind, as she had been after hearing Wilkes's message in his stateroom.

"What did happen?" she asked.

He told her.

It had been just past 7 P.M., local time, of a summer evening in the Northwest Sector of Garnera VI, when the colonists of the distract saw the red light of the flames reflected on the grey-black belly of the low-hanging clouds in the night sky, overhead. But as they had known they were no match for a ship of the Meda V'Dan, they only took to the woods and cowered there until dawn, meanwhile sending a messenger with word of the raid to the next Outpost Station.

So it had been nearly ten o'clock of the bright morning following—for the clouds had cleared with the sunrise—that the outposters from the next station arrived, riding their slide-rafts above the still dew-wet grass to the burned-out station, their heavy, raft-mounted plasma rifles restlessly turning and weaving and searching the sky.

But there had been nothing there for them to find. The ship of the Meda V'Dan had departed with the clouds and the night. And all that had been left where Abruzzi Fifteen Outpost Station had stood were empty warehouses and a burned Residence—charred concrete, smoking, wood ash, and rubble, and among the rubble, a baby, crying.

"Now, why do you suppose they let *him* live?" said one of the station's assistants. He was a lean outposter named Price, who had had his own station once, and lost it to the Meda V'Dan. He spoke sourly.

"Who knows?" retorted Brot Halliday, the station master, scooping up the child—at which, for the moment, the baby voice had cried even more violently. "But he was Chav and Lila's boy, and he's mine now. You'll all be witness to that?"

The three station assistants had nodded. For all its informality, the adoption proceedings, with those nods, became as final as any processed before a judge back on Earth.

"All right for the boy, then," said Price, scowling at the still hot and reeking wood ash, "but the Meda V'Dan have done it and gotten away again in our sector. Picking up after them now won't scare them off from the next time they decide to raid instead of trade!"

"That's our problem, not this boy's," said Brot shortly. "As I say, who knows? Maybe he'll grow up to pay them back in his own way, sometime."

Price had scowled again at the burned-out station. But he said no more on that subject. He had very little respect for the gift of prophecy in any man, but he was too well aware of the strength in Brot's squat body and the shortness of the fuse to Brot's temper to express whatever doubts he may have had about the orphan's future. He had kept his silence, therefore, put the matter from his mind, and done his work during the ensuing years, until he was finally killed during a trading raid on Brot's station by the Meda V'Dan.

As a result of that later raid, the onetime baby, Outposter-Trainee Mark Ten Roos, under tutorship back on faraway Earth, had been gifted on his eighteenth birthday by a message from Outposter HQ, Trinidad, Earth.

The message had been short and to the point, almost brutal in its official language:

Dear Mr. Ten Roos:

It is with great regret that we advise you of information just received here concerning the serious injury of your adopted father during a trading session at his station with ships of the Meda V'Dan, March 32, local calendar, Garnera VI.

Regretfully, Outposter Halliday is not expected to survive; and since the question and estate remain unsettled, it is the recommendation of the Outpost sector commander over his district that you return from Earth at once.

Transportation to Garnera VI is available by civilian spaceship, but may be arranged through this office in the case of station dependents if so preferred . . .

When Mark finished talking, Ulla did not immediately say anything. They walked on together to the end of the corridor and she turned right, Mark following her silently.

"It's all so hard to imagine," she said after a while. "Here Dad's been Outer Navy ever since I was born, and I grew up back in the Earth-City never hearing about anything like that."

"Most people back on Earth don't," said Mark.

"But"—her hand went to the alien trinket at her throat, then dropped away—"it's all so unbelievable, too. I never would have believed someone like Jarl Rakkal would end up being lotteried, for one thing."

"Was he a man who was supposed to have an exemption?"

"No, but somehow it didn't seem as if it could happen to someone on top of the world, like him."

"It usually doesn't," said Mark.

"That's what I mean," she went on innocently. "Nearly everybody who's important has exemption. And most of the people Dad knew were men in the armed services, and of course that gave them automatic exemption as long as they stayed in a career quota of years. And their wives had deferments—"

She reached for the alien cube at her throat again.

"And then," she said, "suddenly nobody seems safe from the lottery anymore, not even me."

He looked down at her profile as they walked together.

"You won't be eligible until you're twenty-five, and not then if you're still in school or training for a career that might produce exemption."

She shook her head—at what, it was not quite clear.

"The colonists," she said suddenly. "Where are they?"

"The colonists on this ship, you mean?" Mark answered. "With the other cargo. In the hold section, aft."

"Twelve-hundred people—back there." Her fingers twisted the chain to the cube. "I'd like to see them."

"They don't let passengers into the cargo section," Mark said. "A safety measure."

"I know. Dad told me." She turned another corner, and now they were headed down a short corridor at the end of which stood a heavy fire door with two Navy enlisted men wearing guard armbands and side arms and carrying rifles. "He said only ship's personnel could get in."

"That's right."

"But—" She looked at him suddenly and caught him studying her. "Outposters—like you—they can go in to see if they want to pick any of the colonists for their own stations. That's true, isn't it?"

"Yes," he said.

"Don't look so grim. I just thought . . ." She hesitated. "You could take me in if you wanted to."

So, he thought, it was this she was after. He felt oddly disappointed to discover it was something so small. He answered brusquely.

"I don't want to."

"Please—" She stopped suddenly, so that he was forced to stop also. She turned to him, taking hold of his right arm persuasively. His left hand came across, swiftly but not roughly, and slid its fingers under hers, breaking their grip.

"Gun arm," he told her. "Never do that."

For a moment she merely stood staring at him, her empty hand still held out towards him, her face pale, her eyes wide.

"Please," she said. "I want to see Jarl. I have to see Jarl!"

"Jarl?"

"Jarl Rakkal. The man I just talked about." She stared at him. "The man you stopped by kicking him into the air, out by the landing stairs when we were coming aboard!"

"That's right," Mark said. "I remember. You did call him Jarl Rakkal. What is he—an old friend of yours?" He made his voice harsh. "Because if that's it, you'd probably be kinder to him, and yourself too, not to try to see him now."

"No, not an old friend," she said, looking up at him, still appealingly. "Oh, we know each other, of course. You keep running into the same people at parties and things. But I can't help feeling for anyone like him—I mean he had so much. He *was* so much. And now he's lost everything."

"So have they all," said Mark.

"Yes, but I don't know them all!" she said swiftly. "I do know him. It isn't just because he's Jarl Rakkal, don't you see? It's because he's somebody I know. I can't just forget he's up there, as part of the . . . cargo. I have to at least try to do something. See him, anyway. Ask him if there isn't some way I can help, some little thing I can do for him . . ."

Her voice ran down and her shoulders sagged. She looked down at the floor.

"But," she said emptily, "you won't take me in."

Yes, thought Mark, looking at her, putting his own hard thoughts against the feeling she seemed to be able to evoke in him, she was undoubtedly clever at getting what she wanted. But there were things he wanted too—things she could not suspect he was after.

"Yes," he said. "On second thoughts, maybe I will take you in. You interest me in the man. I'd like to have another look at him myself."

CHAPTER FOUR

He went forward toward the two guards. She hurried to catch up with him.

"How are they?" he asked the older of the two, a junior petty officer in his mid-thirties.

"Quiet," said the petty officer. "We lost twenty-eight right after lift-off, but we haven't lost one since." He caught sight of the expression on Ulla's face. "Sorry, miss, but it's always like that. It's just after lift-off, when they finally realize nothing's going to stop their going after all, that a lot of them just give up."

"They kill themselves?" Ulla looked sick. "You let them?"

"Just a few—I mean most of the ones we lose just sort of give up and die," said the petty officer. He turned to Mark. "Isn't that right, Outposter? There's nothing we could do even if we wanted to."

"But the others—" she said.

"These men are under orders to leave the others alone," said Mark. "There's no point forcing people to go on living when they don't want to. If you kept them alive now, they'd die shortly after they got to the Colonies, anyway. What's the cycle inside now, guard? Sleep or wake."

"Wake cycle has about another half hour to go," answered the petty officer.

"Get their records," said Mark. "I'd like to look them over."

"Yes, sir."

The petty officer turned to open a panel in the corridor wall and take out a small, brown microfilm box with a viewer screen on its top surface. He handed this to Mark. The other guard was already unlatching the heavy metal dogs locking the fire door. They came loose one by one with soft thumping sounds as they swung back against the sound-absorbent material of the corridor walls. As the last dog dropped loose, the guard swung the door open and the guard who had handed Mark the record file box lifted his rifle to cover the entrance as Mark stepped into it. Ulla pressed hastily in behind him.

"Just a minute, miss." The other guard put his arm across the doorway. "No passengers allowed. I'm sorry."

Mark looked back over his shoulder.

"Tell them who you are," he said to Ulla.

"Ulla Showell," she said. "My father's Admiral-General Jaseth Showell."

"And she'll be under my protection inside there," said Mark. "All right?"

The guard hesitated, then dropped his arms and stood back out of the way.

"Good," said Mark. "Lock the door behind us, then. One of you had better come in and cover us from just inside."

"Yes, sir."

The petty officer, with his rifle at ready, followed as Mark and Ulla stepped through the door into the vast, brightly lighted section of the ship. They stood at the top of a flight of uncarpeted, green-painted metal stairs, looking down into a long dormitory of double-decker bunks ranked side by side in eight long lines parallel to one another, under a ceiling eighty feet in height. Broad aisles between the lines contrasted with the closeness of the double bunks, which had barely five feet of space between them—just enough so that from the high landing where Mark and Ulla stood, they could see down into the spaces between each pair of bunks, right to the space between the last pair of bunks at the far end of the dormitory, where a ceiling-high metal wall put an end to further space.

The top quarter of that wall was taken up by a sign. It was not a temporary sign but a permanent fixture built out from the metal of the wall itself. Its three words were spelled out in letters ten feet high and two feet wide, and shone down on the colonists' area with a light of their own.

ADAPT—OR DIE

Behind Mark, Ulla, and the petty officer the door by which they had entered clashed closed again. There was no soundproofing on this side of it, and the noise of its closing roared and echoed through the colonists' space aboard the *Wombat.*

The sound brought all eyes from below up to the three of them. Men and women, indiscriminately assigned to bunks according to their lottery numbers, looked up from where they stood, sat, or lay, forty feet below, to stare at the intruders from a higher existence they all had once shared equally. Ulla hesitated under the impact of their eyes, but Mark began to descend the open circular staircase leading down to the dormitory floor. After a second she followed.

Most of the conversations below had ceased with the sound of the closing door, but as they went down the circular stairs, the talk picked up gradually until it was a monotonous buzz, echoing steadily below the high, bare-metal ceiling. Before they reached the floor, even the clang of their feet on the stair treads was muffled by the drone of it; which seemed to hang endlessly on the slightly disinfectant-smelling air, like the toneless humming of a man locked and idle in a prison cell.

At the foot of the stairs were two lavatory doors, marked for the different sexes. Mark rapped sharply on each one.

"Back to your bunks, please!" he called.

Taking the records file in his left hand, he went to the aisle between the two lines and began to move down the aisle, glancing at each colonist in turn and checking the records file of his or her personal history, Ulla followed silently behind him.

Conversations that had begun as the two of them descended the stairs died once more as

Mark's eyes came upon the talkers, so that he and Ulla moved in a little travelling circle of silence. For the most part he merely glanced once at a colonist, then at the record file, and moved on to the next individual without a word. But halfway down the aisle he stopped before a middle-aged woman seated on a lower bunk of the row against the wall.

"Position astrophysics?" he asked.

She looked up at him with a grey, lined face in sharp contrast to the black wig she wore.

"That was my husband," she said wearily. "He was a positions officer on one of the Beagrans ships—that's one of the large civilian space shippers."

"But you know something about position calculation?"

"He taught me some," she said. "I had a doctorate in mathematics. It was easy, and when he was away on trips I could plot his probable position shifts for myself and guess pretty close to where he'd be at any given time. It was just something I did when he was away."

Mark nodded. He went down the line.

"You might talk to me," said a voice.

He stopped and looked to his left. Seated cross-legged on an upper bunk was a childlike figure.

"I'm Lily Betaugh," it said. "I was a full professor of philosophy at Belgrade, and I'll do anything to make the best of my situation."

Mark regarded her. Seated on the upper bunk, her face was a little above his, and he was close enough so that he could see the

faint marks of beginning crow's-feet at the
corners of the eyes in the childishly round
face.

"What do you know about the Meda
V'Dan?" he asked.

"Very little," Lily said. "I don't think any
human knows much, except that they trade
with us and with the Unknown Races of aliens
farther in toward Galactic Centre. If they've
got a written philosophy, I don't know about
it, and that makes me doubt their claim that
they're more advanced than we are."

"A lot of the technology's more advanced."

"Stone Age savages," she said, "can fire
plasma rifles. But being able to use and being
able to build are two different things."

Mark looked at her curiously for a moment.

"Perhaps," he said. He moved on.

Ulla followed him as he worked his way
down one aisle and up the next. Every so often
he stopped to question one of the colonists,
usually about some particular skill of knowledge they were recorded as possessing. He
talked to a number of men and women who
had picked up mechanical skills as the result
of some hobby or other, an industrial chemist,
a bookkeeper, two men and one woman
whose avocations had been gourmet cookery,
a male ballet dancer, and a brown, wiry little
man whose hobby had been butterfly collect-
ing. The only one, however, to whom he held
out any hope of being chosen for his colony
was a man named Orag Spal, who had been a
Marine non-commissioned gun-control officer
for twenty-three years before a dishonourable

discharge for theft cast him out of the protection of the armed services, three years short of the retirement that would have ensured his lifetime exemption from the lottery.

"You could never be an outposter," Mark said to Spal bluntly. "We wouldn't have you if you could. But you still can be the next thing to it if you're willing to work. How about it?"

"I'm willing," said Spal. He lay at full length on a lower bunk, a short, thick-shouldered man with hair only starting to grey. "I'll give you as much as I've got."

"All right," said Mark. He pressed a button on the records file that marked Spal's dossier. "I've punched you for my station. You may have to go to the general yards on Garnera Six with the rest when the ship lands, but eventually you'll come to me."

He went on. And in due time he came to Jarl Rakkal.

Jarl, like the Marine, was lying on his back on a lower bunk when they came to him. Unlike Spal, the big man's frame filled the bunk to overflowing and his dark blue boots rested with their ankles on the foot bar on his bunk, the feet and sole projecting into the aisles. The bunk seemed doll-bed sized beneath him. Ulla pushed past Mark to go to the head of the lower bunk and Jarl shifted his wide shoulders aside to make a narrow space on the bunk's edge.

"Ulla Showell!" he said. "Sit down."

"Hello, Jarl," she said softly, accepting his invitation. He looked past her to Mark, standing at the foot of the bunk with the records file box in his hand.

"Outposter, sir," Jarl said, smiling a little. "You're a good man. I came close to caving in your chest outside the ship there, sir."

"Jarl!" said Ulla. "His name is Mark Ten Roos. You don't have to call him sir."

"I might as well start getting used to it, though," Jarl said. He lifted his eyebrows at Mark. "Shouldn't I?"

"It's not going to make any difference," Mark said.

"Isn't it?" Jarl said. "Then I'll drop the sir for the moment, Mr. Ten Roos. Any time you change your mind, let me know."

"Jarl!" Ulla looked unhappy. "It's not natural for you to be like this."

"I'm not being like anything, honey-girl," said Jarl, looking at her. The sound of the upper-class pet name jarred on Mark's ears. "I'm not being like anything at all. I'm just being what I actually am now—a colonist. I've got a few more brains than to waste any emotion on the past, now that it's gone for good. I'm just out to make the most of the future."

"You can call it a future!" said Ulla. She looked ready to cry.

"As long as I'm alive, it's a future," said Jarl. He glanced at the back wall of the colonists' section to the huge sign with its unsparing message. "And I'm planning on staying alive. I understand you outposters sometimes take your pick of us colonists for your own stations, Mr. Ten Roos. Want to pick me?"

"What do you know?" Mark asked.

"*Ki*, most sports, publishing, people and

how to handle them," Jarl said. "But mostly I'm just better than most of these you see around you. Bigger, brighter, tougher—that much more for your money. I'm a fast learner, also a self-starter. I can work on my own without supervision, and I'm ambitious —but I know when to keep the ambitions under control."

Mark consulted the records file.

"Banking?" he asked.

Jarl flicked a big hand upward momentarily.

"My family's been in it for generations. I grew up with it," he said. "So, I had to absorb a lot of it through my skin during my first sixteen years or so. If you really want a banker, I can try to summon up some old ghosts, and re-educate myself."

He stopped and smiled again at Mark.

"It's the first I heard of them having banks out in the Colonies, though," he said.

"They haven't," answered Mark. He dropped the records file to his side and looked at Ulla.

"Can't you give me a few minutes?" she demanded. "Can't you leave us alone for just a minute or two?"

Mark shook his head.

"You're under my protection," he answered.

"Jarl can protect me."

Jarl laughed.

"Honey-girl," he said. "I'm one of the ones he's protecting you from. No, don't look so shocked. How do you know what I wouldn't be willing to do if it meant making me better off as a colonist?"

"You wouldn't . . . " She let the sentence run off.

"You're wrong," Jarl said softly. "Oh, you're wrong. And the outposter's right. As it happens, you'd be safe all right with me—not only from me but from any of these other colonists as long as I was with you. But he's got no way of knowing that, and he's too good at his own job to take a chance on me, and that's right."

Ulla looked grimly at Mark.

"All right," she said. She turned and, bending down her head, began to talk with Jarl in whispers too low for Mark to overhear.

Mark waited patiently. The slow second hand of his watch crawled around its dial. Suddenly the overhead lights in the colonists' section faded to a glow-worm flicker.

"Sleep cycle." An amplified voice spoke from overhead. "Beginning of the eight-hour sleep cycle. Keep all noise and movement to a minimum, please."

Jarl sat up in the shadowed dimness of his lower cot, gently pushing Ulla off, onto her feet.

"End of interview," he said. "Mr. Ten Roos is ready to leave. Look, we don't want to do anything that'll make him not want me for his station."

Ulla turned toward Mark, smoothing her face into an expression at least neutral if not congenial. She stepped out between the bunks and turned right in the aisle, toward the bottom of the spiral staircase. Mark turned after her.

"Just one thing, Mr. Ten Roos, if you don't mind," said Jarl behind him.

Mark stopped and looked back.

Jarl nodded toward the big letters of the sign on the wall, still glowing with their own separate light above the twelve hundred colonists, then looked back at Mark.

"Remember—I'm going to live," said Jarl softly. "One of the ones who does."

Mark left him and followed Ulla down the dim aisle. They mounted the twisting metal stairs to the landing, where the petty officer had the door already open, waiting for them.

Back once more in the passenger section of the ship, they walked away together in silence, until a turn in the corridor hid them from the two Navy guards. Then Ulla stopped and turned to face Mark, leaning back tiredly against the corridor wall.

"You might as well know," she said. "Dad will do it if I ask. He's got a few civilian employees at Navy Base, in his Blue One Command. They do maintenance on the obsolete ships the Outer Navy has mothballed there in case of emergency damage to the regular fleet. I talked it over with Jarl, and we both decided to ask Dad to pull strings to get Jarl assigned as a maintenance man. With millions of colonists being shipped off Earth every year, they won't turn down Dad's asking for just one. You don't have to help us—just don't tell Dad you got me in to talk to Jarl. Just promise you won't hinder."

She almost put her hands appealingly on his gun arm again, but remembered in time and dropped them back to her sides. Mark gazed at her. No one could be this good an actress. On the other hand, it was incredible that anyone could be so ignorant of the machinery that controlled all their lives—Earth-Citians, outposters, and colonists alike.

"No," he said slowly.

"No?" Her eyes widened, and she stepped back from him. "You don't mean you *will* hinder?"

"I would if I thought I needed to," said Mark. "But I don't. It won't work. You ought to know that's one string not even an admiral-general of the Blue can pull."

"He can't?" she echoed. "You mean Dad can't get *one* colonist—just one man?"

"Of course not," said Mark. "You can buy almost anything back on Earth, but the one thing that's not for sale anywhere is the Earth-City's own survival. Even one man is too many. One man's a precedent, and there aren't going to be any precedents for colonists escaping once they've been lotteried. Earth wants these people gone—for good and without recourse. There's no single individual on Earth the Earth-City wouldn't sacrifice to make sure the excess population it bleeds off stays bled."

She blinked at him unbelievingly.

"You—" She ran out of words. "What've you got against Jarl? Why are you picking on him, out of all of them, like this?"

"I'm not," Mark said. "I'm only somewhat

better educated than you seem to be. I'm also
a better judge of men. Your friend Jarl knew
there wasn't any hope in this maintenance-
man idea of yours. It was his idea, wasn't it?—
for you to mention it to me."

"Why . . . yes," she said. "He thought—"

"He thought, or maybe you both thought, I
might be touched at seeing you cook up such a
hopeless scheme," said Mark. "Rakkal must
know better than to guess I'd be concerned
about him alone. But he could have hoped I
might just be concerned enough about you to
add one name to my list of colonists. What's
one man among millions, you said? Well,
what's one man among thousands? And there
are thousands at the station I'll be taking
over."

He smiled at her again, and this time there
was no doubt the smile was bitter.

"Tell me," he said. "That phrase about the
one man among millions—that was his
suggestion too, wasn't it?"

She exploded suddenly.

"But you hate him—or me!" she cried. "You
must, or you wouldn't be like this." Her
hands were clenched into fists, and they
quivered helplessly as if she longed to use
them upon him, but dared not. "*Why* are you
like this? There's no reason! Why?"

"There's a reason," he said, and sighed.
With that sigh, the bitterness flowed out of
him, leaving him empty and resigned. "I'm a
disposable—as you said outside the ship—literally a disposable item on the human
balance sheets. But you wouldn't understand

that any more than anyone else does. Don't worry, I'll take Jarl Rakkal to my station. But for my reasons, not his—or yours."

"You . . . will?"

The unexpected victory was so powerful in its effect on her that she looked at him with unbelieving eyes, hands opening and falling limp.

He nodded coldly, taking refuge from the effect of those eyes of hers in the memory of the purpose that had dominated him as long as he could remember.

It did not matter who Ulla was, he reminded himself, or that she could manage to stir him as she did. Nothing mattered, as long as he could use her, or anyone else who came to hand, to do what needed to be done.

Therefore, it did not matter, either, if she were the spoiled child of wealth and power he had taken her to be at first or whether she were an honestly uninformed idealist who really cared whether a man she had known should be left to scratch for a living in some nameless colony, with no hope of ever regaining what he had lost.

The facts were the only things that mattered. The fact that the Space Navy was rotten with a do-nothing spirit; the fact that the Earth was deliberate in its selfish indifference to the colonists it deported to maintain its own artificial standard of living; the fact that Jarl Rakkal was an example of the worst of Earth in that same selfish indifference, caring for nothing but himself and of use to no one but himself, unless some stronger hand

took him like a tool and put him to work; the
fact that her own father was as corrupt as any
other admiral-general in the Space Navy.

It might be, he thought unexpectedly, that
she was aware of these things, but still trying
to deny them. As if by some means she could
find a way to put nobility back into men like
Rakkal and her father, and the whole Earth-
City/Colonies arrangement. Yes, Mark told
himself now, a little surprised at how true
this new insight rang in him, that was the
most likely explanation for Ulla. She was
obviously the kind that would cling with tooth
and nail to anything or anyone she was deter-
mined to save, in the face of all the facts.

"You *will?*" she was demanding again now,
since he had not answered immediately.

He shook off his speculation, reminding
himself once again that whatever she really
was did not matter.

"That's right," he said flatly, "but not for
nothing. It's interesting you mentioned that
maintenance situation at Navy Base. I've got
my own price for picking Jarl Rakkal, and it's
a high one. But one you can actually get your
father to pay, and one where the strings he
pulls will work."

CHAPTER FIVE

The man on the bed was little more than half a man. Brot Halliday's right leg was gone just below the knee, his left leg almost at the hip. His left arm was missing below the elbow, and the right side of his face and body were just beginning to recover from the temporary paralysis from the corona of the Meda V'Dan fire weapon that had crippled his two legs and one arm. He was supposed to have been dying, but he had not. He had refused, and now the physician that the Navy had sent out to deal with him had endorsed that refusal. It was the physician's conclusion that Brot Halliday would live—for the forseeable future at least.

"Mark . . ." Brot's words were a little blurred with weakness, but strong enough to be heard. He looked up at Mark's face above him, at the side of the bed. "They wanted to put me away and leave the station up for grabs. Hell, no. This is going to be your station, and I'll hold it for you until you're ready to take over . . . ."

The burst of energy that had allowed him to string three sentences together into a single speech played out suddenly, and his voice left him. He lay, trying to get his vocal cords back into action again, the muscles in his still-thick neck working.

"Don't talk," said Mark. He had been holding Brot's paralyzed right hand. Now he put it gently back under the bedcover and let go of it. "Plenty of time for that when you're stronger. I brought you some presents. Let me take you outside and show you."

Mark reached up to touch the autocontrols at the head of the bed. The motors beneath it whirred alive, and the bed floated through the bedroom door on its air cushion, slid across the living room and out the front door of the Residence, into the cool air of early spring of the north temperate zone of Garnera VI.

"Look," said Mark. He pressed the button that raised the head of the bed, so that Brot could look forward. The balding round skull was lifted, the hard brown eyes stared out over the square quarter mile of cleared landing area before the Residence and the other buildings of the Outpost Station now in the process of reconstruction. There, spaced about the area, were four small squat Navy spaceships, tail down, nose up, and looking ready to lift at a moment's notice.

"The Navy here? What the hell?" whispered Brot.

"Not the Navy," said Mark. "They're ours— mothballed heavy scout ships, released to me on lease to help scare away any Meda V'Dan who might think of hitting us again here at Station Fourteen before we've gotten back our full strength.''

Brot stared at the gleaming shapes of the obsolete warcraft. Then, slowly, his chest began to heave. It heaved several times like a bellows working up to full inflation, before the fruits of its effort came forth in a series of short hoarse coughs that were actually laughter.

''Lower me down . . .'' he whispered, exhausted, when the paroxysm had run its course. ''Scarecrow Navy . . . really . . . playing . . . scarecrow, after all . . . Mark, you . . . boy . . .''

At that point, he literally did run out of the capacity for speech, and Mark wheeled him back inside to the bedroom. There, Brot spent the better part of an hour building up both his strength and his verbal capacity, before ordering Mark to drive the hospital bed into the Residence planning room for a meeting with the other outposters, those under Brot's command at Station Fourteen.

The four of them were there waiting when Mark and Brot finally came in—Horace Hubble, the assistant station master, and three senior grade outposters, the youngest of them six years older than Mark.

''All right,'' said Brot, when his bed was wheeled into position before the chairs on which they sat waiting, ''here's Mark. And you know . . . what I want you to do. You'll take orders from him, from now on. Even though on the rolls he's junior to all . . . of you.''

Brot's voice ran out into a barely audible whisper and fell silent.

"I thought so," said Stein Chamoy.

He got to his feet. He was a tall, rawboned outposter, almost as big as Jarl Rakkal, and second in authority after Horace Hubble at Station Fourteen.

"Sit down, Stein," said Horace, for Brot's neck was working as he struggled to speak.

"Sorry, Race," said Stein, looking at him. He looked back at Brot. "And I'm sorry, Brot. Quit trying to split yourself to talk, damn it! You know how I felt about this. I hung on this long hoping you wouldn't try to go through with it."

"Don't like . . . get out . . . " whispered Brot.

"That's what I'm going to do," said Stein. He turned to the doorway of the planning room. "I'll either retire or take a transfer. Let you know in the morning."

"Hold it," said Race Hubble. He was a thin, gangling, long-armed brown man, with arm and leg joints that looked as loose as a marionette's. "You may not want to take orders from Mark, Stein, but you'll take them from me as long as you're on the rolls at this station. Just hold up a minute. Maybe we can talk this thing out."

"There's nothing to talk out," said Stein, looking back at Race. He stopped, however, and glanced once more at Brot and Mark. "Unless Brot wants to change his mind."

"I'll see you . . ."

"Easy Brot," said Race. "Let's all stay easy about this. You've got to admit it's not a normal thing to put four experienced men under the authority of a boy just out of school, with no experience at all."

"I say . . ."

"No," Mark put his hand on Brot's good shoulder, to calm the older man. "Let me talk to them, Brot. Stein, you were here at the station when Brot carried me home. You know me."

"I know you, Mark. I like you for that matter, boy," said Stein. "But there are twenty-four hundred plus colonists in my quadrant that need a real station master here at the Outpost to keep them alive and healthy. If I can't give them that, anything else I can give them isn't worth having. You may be hell on wheels someday. Mark, but right now you're just another green kid fresh from Earth with your head full of book learning, and my colonists—your colonists, Mark—can't eat books when the winter comes. As I say, I want out."

"Wait—" Race Hubble began again, as Stein turned away.

"No, Race," Mark said, "let him go. If he's made up his mind, then he's not going to listen to me no matter what I tell him. His mind's already closed. I wouldn't be able to use him. Or"—he looked around at Orval Belothen and Paul Trygve, the other two outposters—"anyone else who's got a closed mind."

Orval Belothen, a short, round-faced outposter in his early thirties, shifted in his chair and looked at the floor of the planning room, Paul Trygve, slim, dark-haired, and twenty-eight years old, stared straight back at Mark, but with a narrow frown line between his level brows.

"That's settled, then," said Stein. He headed for the door.

"Only," Mark said after him, and Stein hesitated, looking back, "you might want to make it a transfer instead of retirement, Stein. Just in case a year from now you change your mind about me?"

For a second more, Stein hesitated.

"Maybe. All right, a transfer," he said. And went.

"All right," said Mark to the three who were left. He pulled up a chair for himself and sat down. They faced one another in a rough circle, four men in chairs and one in a floating hospital bed. "I'll tell you why I'm taking what Brot's offered me, and when I'm done if any more of you want to transfer, that's up to you. Stein's right. I'm a green kid fresh from Earth; moreover, I'm a green kid who spent my first thirteen years out here and knows that there's no substitute for experience when you're an outposter. But I've happened to come back out at a time when the whole structure of things is ready to break down. Any of you know what I'm talking about?"

He looked around at them. They all looked back wordlessly.

"I didn't really expect you to," Mark said. "The only place it can really be seen is from Earth. But it's plain enough if you look at it from there. Briefly, the whole Colonies plan is reaching the point where it's ready to collapse of its own weight."

"This is *your* idea, Mark?" asked Race.

"It's the idea of a number of scholars who've taken the trouble to dig into the situation—like a man named Wilkes Danielson, who was my tutor on Earth-City. The trouble is, a man like Wilkes can talk his head off and everyone listens because of his reputation. But no one remembers what he says for five minutes, because they'd rather they'd never heard it in the first place."

"Mark," said Orval Belothen, "are you planning to bet this Outpost and its colony and all of us on some theory dreamed up by bookworms away back on Earth-City, where they don't know anything about conditions out here anyway, and don't want to know?"

"It's no bet, Orv," said Mark. "It's a case of a volcano exploding, sooner or later, and whether we're making up our minds to move now or to wait until we see the hot lava bearing down on us."

Orv nodded, but he sat back in his chair, plucking at his lower lip. Mark turned to Paul Trygve.

"How about you, Paul?"

"I'm listening," said the youngest of the station's regular outposters.

"Then I'll get into it." Mark leaned forward in his chair. "I brought those scout ships outside for a number of reasons. But one of them was to prove something of what I'm saying. I got them all—four ships worth maybe twenty million in credits—for doing a single small favour for the admiral-general of the Blue. I agreed to include one colonist, on request, in my choices from a shipped batch, for our station here. Four ships for one colonist. Stop and think about that for a second. That's how worm-eaten the Navy's getting."

He paused.

"What's this colonist got?" Orv exploded.

"Jaseth Showell's daughter likes him," said Mark.

Orv looked at Race, at Brot, and over at Paul.

"I can't believe it," he said.

"Do you believe it?" Mark demanded.

Orv hesitated, shook his head a little, then nodded.

"I'll believe you—if you're sure you know what you're talking about, Mark," he said.

"I was the one who made the trade with Showell," said Mark.

Slowly, Orv nodded again.

"All right, then," said Mark. "The Navy's gone rotten. The Earth-City's gone rotten. The colonist system is breaking down. The Meda V'Dan are getting more uncontrolled every day—look at their attacking a five-man Outpost station like this. Ten years ago, they'd never have risked anything so open or on such a scale. They'd have known that the Navy would have had to retaliate. Now they know they can do something like this and the Navy won't send out a single ship to hunt down the aliens who did it. How about it, Orv? Am I right about that or not?"

Orv looked grimly at him.

"You're right, as far as the Meda V'Dan and

the Navy go nowadays, anyway," he said. "All right, Mark. Let's have the whole story. I'm listening."

"It's simple enough," said Mark. "The Colonies system is gradually bankrupting the Earth-City economically. In theory this shouldn't be happening. In theory the older colonies by this time should be self-supporting, freeing supplies, equipment, and outposters to work with the newer Colonies. It hasn't worked out that way, though, because the plan was rotten at the core to begin with."

"Now, wait—" Orv said.

"Wait yourself, Orv," said Mark. "You know it was. The theory was that since not enough people were emigrating Earth voluntarily to hold the population there down to workable limits, we have a lottery—an absolutely fair and square lottery that would force emigration of the necessary number of people purely on a chance basis."

"It was a good theory," put in Paul, "particularly for the situation at that time, a hundred years ago. Something had to be done fast."

"True enough," said Mark, looking at Paul, "only it hasn't worked out. In practice, they needed experts to guide the amateur colonists —us outposters. They needed an armed force to protect them—the Space Navy. And the people manning those organizations had to be exempt from the lottery. So did necessary Earth government figures. So did certain people necessary to the running of the Earth-City, and so on. No wonder it has all ended up just the way it has. The lottery gets its pick all right—but only of the human garbage of Earth. And garbage doesn't make very good colonists. Which means that Colonies founded nearly a hundred years ago still aren't able to run themselves without outposters, or survive without supply shipments, or face the Meda V'Dan without either the Navy or us to fight for them."

"It was still a sound idea to begin with," said Orv.

"It never was sound. It was rotten. It was basically selfish," said Mark. "It was a plan with the essential unspoken purpose of making the Earth-City safe and sweet and uncrowded for an intellectual and political aristocracy that was immune to the lottery."

Paul laughed softly.

"A good thing Stein left," the young outposter said. "He'd be calling you out right now, Mark, as too dangerous a radical to live."

"If Stein would think it through, he'd realize he's as much of a radical as I am," Mark said. "The system victimizes outposters as much as it victimizes the colonists. That's not the point, though. The point is that it's because the system was selfish to begin with and therefore rotten in practice that it's finally beginning to smash itself up."

"You said that to begin with," Paul said. "But you still haven't said how it's smashing up."

"Simple," said Mark. "The Colonies aren't becoming self-supporting because the colonists didn't want to emigrate in the first place and because they're culls to begin with —adults only, twenty-five to eighty years old, most of them people who've already failed in the society they were born into. People like that are the material for colonizing new worlds? The Colonies aren't growing up to stand on their own, but they're multiplying every week. And the cost of supplying them, us, and the Navy is beginning to get out of hand."

"Mark," said Orv, "I don't believe that. The Earth-City's not starving. It's a long way from starving."

"No," said Paul. "There's maybe a thirty percent slack in production that can be taken out—or at least that's the way the figures ran when I left Earth six years ago—but then we'll be hitting about maximum output back there."

"Thirty percent," said Orv. "That means we can add damn near a third again as many colonies before feeling pinched. That could take another thirty years to do. I don't see that as much of an emergency."

"It won't take thirty years," said Mark. "We've got the Meda V'Dan helping to wreck the situation now."

Orv opened his mouth, then closed it again. He sat back in his chair.

"Eighteen years ago, when my parents were killed," Mark said, looking at all of them around the room, "the Meda V'Dan hit only an occasional small, two-outposter station like theirs with a single ship, so that the rest of the aliens could claim the raiders were renegades. How many Meda V'Dan ships did it take to cut you up here at Fourteen last month?"

"Six . . . six, God damn . . ." husked Brot.

"There you are," said Mark. "When they start hitting five-man stations, and with half fleets, the old excuse about renegades is getting stretched pretty well beyond believability. But you ought to know why they aren't worried about that as well as I do."

He looked at Orv.

"The Navy's no threat any more. Sure. Those fat-bellies . . ." Orv took time to swear. "I'll go along with you on that, Mark."

"All right, then, there it is," said Mark. "The Meda V'Dan hardly bother to trade anymore. They take what they want from Earth-produced supplies at the Outpost Stations and keep the Navy quiet with gifts from the Unknown Races farther on—only the gifts aren't worth two percent of what it takes. The Navy takes the gifts and covers up, because it doesn't want to fight. And the responsible people back on Earth help with the cover-up because they don't want the Navy to fight, either. Earth is beginning to get scared of the Meda V'Dan. It's only a matter of time before they find an excuse to haul the Navy back to the Solar System for their own protection and start paying flat-out tribute to the Meda V'Dan. And that's going to be the beginning of the end. Because once the Meda V'Dan start taking from Earth, direct, they'll suck her dry."

"And," said Paul quietly, "we'll be left out here alone with the colonists—and no supplies."

Mark looked at him.

"If you were on my side from the first, Paul," he said, "why didn't you say so?"

"I wanted to see what kind of argument you'd put up," Paul said. "Also, I wanted to be sure you could get through to Orv and Race, here, without me."

Mark looked at the two older outposters.

"Right, Mark," said Race, "we'll take your orders—for a while anyway—and see how things work out. Or maybe I shouldn't speak for Orv?"

He looked across at the round-bodied man.

"You can talk for me," said Orv. "I'm convinced. Only, what've you got in mind, Mark?"

"To begin with, making this Outpost and this colony self-sufficient," said Mark. "No, more than just self-sufficient. Independent. The colonists I picked on the trip out should be here in a few days. Meanwhile, I want a general check of local colonists' records for special skills, then I'll have a talk with our Wild Bunch."

CHAPTER SIX

The dozen or so colonists Mark had chosen from those aboard the *Wombat* came in by shuttle ship from the processing centre on Garnera VI two days later. Among them were Jarl Rakkal and Lily Betaugh. Also, the ex-Marine Orag Spal, Age Hammerschold, and the woman with the black wig who had made a hobby out of position astrophysics.

It was with this woman, whose name was Maura Vols, that Mark concerned himself first. He took her on a private tour of one of the formerly mothballed heavy scout ships the Navy had leased Station Fourteen. The tour ended in the navigator's compartment.

It was a tiny cubicle of a room, its walls packed with controls and metering devices.

"Can you handle this equipment?" Mark asked her bluntly.

She revolved about in the centre of the room, staring at her surroundings.

"I don't understand ten percent of it," she said. "I used my husband's position tables and rental time on a commercial computer."

But the tone of her voice was at odds with the defeatism of her words, and two spots of colour had come to life on her pale cheeks.

"I could try to figure it all out, of course," she said. "Everything here has to tie in some-where with what I learned from Tom."

"Do that, then," said Mark. "And when you can make it all work for you, check with the colony personnel records. Pick out the four people with the best mathematical back-ground for learning what you've got to teach. Then let me know, and I'll see they're assign-ed to you."

He also took Orag Spal on a tour of the four ships, with particular attention to the two fixed million-pound rifles, mounted fore and aft in each.

"First, are they workable?" Mark asked the ex-Marine. "Second, can you train men to handle them? And I mean handle them effec-tively, in action."

"Oh, they'll work," Spal said. "The only thing is, either one of them could suck the engines on one of these little boats dry if you fire it when the craft's not on balance or power is off. As for training men to handle them, give me the right kind of man and time enough, I'll train him."

"What's the right kind of man?"

"Good reflexes. Endurance. Teachable. Young, by preference." Spal looked sideways and up at Mark. "But colonists being all over twenty-five—and most of that crowd I came out with were a good deal over—I suppose we'll have to skip that."

"Not necessarily," said Mark. "We've got some second-and-third generation young people, particularly among a sort of semirebel group called the Wild Bunch, who might fit your requirements exactly. I'll be talking to them in a day or so."

"Good," Spal said. "Meanwhile I'll get busy tearing these choppers down for close inspection."

Mark went off to turn his attention to Lily Betaugh. He had arranged for her and Jarl Rakkal to be housed at the Outpost itself, instead of in the nearest quadrant village with the other colonists. Now he took her to the library and records sections of the Outpost, which, being underground, had escaped the fire and destruction of the Meda V'Dan raid that had destroyed nearly all the other Outpost buildings except the Residence itself.

"It's a fairly good general library," he said. "But more important, it has a hundred years of this colony's history, including a lot of general information over those years about the actions of the Meda V'Dan where the Colonies were concerned. Find yourself the best ex-psychologist, ex-sociologist, and ex-anthropologist among those listed in the colonists' records, and get them to help you. I want a race profile of the Meda V'Dan as well as you can work it up, including probable prehistoric evolution, present philosophy, and society."

She nodded.

"You realize, though," she said, "there's no

reason we should come up with any more information than you could get by stepping over to that encyclopedia right now and coding for its section on the Meda V'Dan?"

He smiled.

"The information about the Meda V'Dan in that encyclopedia, or any encyclopedia back on Earth, is ninety percent guesswork, and ninety percent of that guesswork is wrong," he answered. "Study the colony's history, just as I said. You'll find out in a hurry that it and the encyclopedia don't correlate."

He turned at last to Jarl Rakkal, since Age Hammerschold, the one ordinary-choice colonist he had picked from those aboard the *Wombat*, had been assigned to the colony's one semisuccessful furniture manufactory.

"Here," he said, leading the big man, now dressed in colonist's green work slacks and shirt, into the half-rebuilt comptroller's building behind the Residence, "this is where you'll be working. We lost a good share of the records, but duplicates of the copies sent to Sector Headquarters for this planet will be coming in to replace them in the next few days."

Jarl looked around him, half amused, half puzzled.

"But what am I supposed to do here?" he asked.

"Set up profit-making systems for the colony, and see that the systems work," said Mark. "In particular, find me something right away that we can use to trade directly with the Meda V'Dan."

Jarl stared at him.

"You don't mean this?"

"Didn't you tell me you came from a banking family?" said Mark. "Weren't you the owner of a publishing business at the time you were lotteried?"

"Of course," said Jarl. He stared for a moment longer at Mark. "But, Mr. Ten . . . look, can I call you Mark?"

"Go ahead," said Mark.

"All right, Mark, forgive me if it sounds like I'm telling you what to do, instead of the other way around," Jarl said. "But I started the most successful parti-fax publishing outlet the Earth-City's ever seen, from scratch. At the time the lottery got me, I had nearly a hundred and fifty million repro outfits in as many homes and offices—nearly a billion customers, by estimate, making up their daily reading from my broadcast items. I did all that in six years—with plenty of time out for *ki* practice and everything else I wanted to do. Look at me. I may not be able to handle one of your outposter professionals, but I'll bet that out of ten thousand or so colonists you've got attached to this station, there's not a man who can stay in a locked room with me for three minutes and come out on his feet."

He paused, staring at Mark.

"And you still want to use me as a sort of glorified bookkeeper?"

"If that's the way you want to describe it," said Mark, "yes."

"But—" Rakkal broke off. "Forgive me again if I sound offensive or patronizing—

God knows I'm in no position to patronize anyone now, let alone you—but believe me, this one time I'm being completely honest with you when I say you can't mean to waste the sort of raw material I am on a job like that. I'm a few years older than you, and maybe it takes a few more years than you've got to realize what someone like me, with my experience, could do for you. For example, I gather you might be trying to actually use those scout ships you got from the Navy. Fine, that's the way I like to think myself. Now, I've piloted civilian craft almost that size—''

''No,'' said Mark. He met Rakkal's eyes squarely. ''You're too ambitious. I wouldn't trust you to operate a tractor out of my sight.''

''But you're putting the whole economy of this Outpost and colony in my hands?''

''Exactly,'' said Mark.

He went toward the door of the building, which was at the moment only a door by courtesy—a raw, new frame of wood, open to the outer air on two sides and overhead. Jarl called after him.

''What if I deliberately mess things up?''

''If the colony starves, you do, too,'' said Mark. ''Remember, find me something I can trade to the Meda V'Dan—do that right away.''

He went out.

It took the rest of the week to round up the Wild Bunch from their various caves and forests and the homes of relatives in the villages of the colony's four sections who were not supposed to be giving the nonworkers food and shelter, but were. However, the morning finally came when Mark spoke to about a hundred and twenty of the bunch, mostly men dressed in everything from tattered green work clothes to animal skins, in the landing area surrounded by the four heavy Navy scout ships.

"All right," said Mark. He was standing up on the front seat of a ground car to be seen better by them all. "Each one of you knows why you're here. You're the colony mavericks, and I'm not going to waste much time on you. This afternoon I'm going to start going around to the quadrant villages, telling the rest of the people what this colony's going to do. You here are getting an advanced briefing because the bare chance exists that you can be particularly useful—if you want to be."

They looked back at him. Their faces were not encouraging.

"I'm going to make this colony independent," said Mark. "Not just independent of supplies from Earth, but independent of Earth, Navy Base, and even the other Colonies in our sector on this planet. But the changeover's not going to be easy. We'll probably go hungry this winter, for one thing. I don't think we'll have to fight the Navy, but we'll probably have to fight the Meda V'Dan—and for once this means that you colonists are going to be in on the fighting. It's not going to be just the outposters alone."

"Why should we?" asked an unidentified

voice from the crowd. Paul and Orv, standing by, with thumbs hooked in their gun belts, ran their eyes over the crowd, but it was impossible to say who had spoken.

"To make that better life you all claim you've been after," replied Mark. "You're our rebels. I'm giving you a chance to lead the rebellion of the whole colony against the system we've been trapped by out here for nearly a hundred years. We're going to become a real colony—self-supporting and self-protecting. But I'm not forcing any of you to go along with this unless you want to. Those who aren't interested can go back to wherever you were when we found you, but it's only fair to warn you that if you've been depending on relatives, you may not find them as generous, once things start to change around here."

He pointed to the scout ships.

"I need younger men to man these ships," he said. "I need older men to help me and the other outposters lead the rest of the colonists into the changes we have to make. I can't offer any of you anything for this—except that once we get the changes made, there won't be any distinction between us as colonists and outposters anymore. We'll all be colonists of Abruzzi Fourteen together, and whoever can lead us best will be our leaders."

He paused. They looked at him in silence.

"Well, then," he said, "it's up to you. Those who want no part of it, take off now. Those who want to lead or enlist in the Abruzzi Colony Space Navy, gather around the car here."

The crowd slowly began to move. It broke up into two movements, a movement of perhaps a third of those there toward the ground car and a dispersal of the rest in all directions.

"Good," said Mark, for though the large majority of those present were leaving, almost all of those under twenty were among the group that was staying. "All right. Paul and Orv will list you and what you volunteer to do. Those who want to work with the scout ships will find an ex-Marine named Orag Spal in that ship to the right, there. He'll start training you. The rest of you follow me up to the Residence so that I can explain the individual jobs that need to be done, and then you'll join me in my swing around the villages to talk to the rest of the colonists this afternoon—"

The chiming of the phone in the ground car interrupted him; he reached down to pick it up.

"Mark," he said into it.

Brot's labouring voice spoke back to him.

"Mark . . . send Orv, Paul, here."

"Send Orv and Paul?" Mark frowned at the phone. "Brot, what're you doing, calling out like this? What do you want Orv and Paul for?"

"Just . . . send . . ."

The phone clicked out of communication. Mark looked over at the other two outposters and found their troubled glance upon him.

"What's this?" Mark asked. "Brot's calling for both of you. Do either of you know anything about this?"

Paul's face was sombre.

"It's my fault," he said.

"No," said Orv. "It was all three of us who decided to do it."

"But it was my idea," said Paul. "Mark, it must be Stein up at the Residence. I thought if he had a look at how things were going, he might change his mind. I asked him to come back out from Sector Headquarters to look, before his transfer request went through. Race was to show him around while you were busy with the bunch, here—"

"Orv," said Mark, dropping down into the seat behind the controls of the ground car, "you take care of them here. Paul, come on with me."

Paul took three strides and a running jump to join him in the ground car. Mark set the vehicle in motion, swung it about on the grass, and sent it sliding swiftly toward the Residence, only a few hundred yards away.

CHAPTER SEVEN

They burst into Brot's bedrom to see Race lying still on the carpet, Stein behind him, standing with his back against a wall and his arms crossed on his chest, hands on opposite shoulders. In the bed, half sitting, Brot held a gun in his one hand, resting the butt on his knee, the barrel pointed at Stein.

"Cover Stein!" snapped Mark to Paul.

He stepped quickly to the bed and took the gun from Brot. Brot's face was white with exhaustion and he sagged back against his pillows as the gun left his hand. But the exhaustion had not reached that grim inner core of his.

"Told you . . ." he whispered to Mark, "send Paul, Orv . . . not come . . . self . . ."

"Easy, Brot," said Mark.

He turned and went to the still figure of Race, but as he knelt by the downed man, Race stirred and tried to sit up, putting a hand to his head.

"I just gun-whipped him," said Stein. "He'll

be all right except for a headache."

Mark got to his feet, facing Stein. "What happened?"

"I gave Brot a chance to take charge at the station here, again," Stein said. "He told Race to take my gun. I clipped Race instead. Turned out Brot had a gun under his pillow."

Race was on his feet now, if somewhat unsteady there. He turned to Stein.

"Sorry, Race," Stein said. "Seems we've ended up on different sides after all."

Race reached for the gun in his own holster.

"Never mind," said Mark swiftly. Race's hand fell to his side. "Insubordination . . ." whispered Brot. "Shoot, Paul . . ."

"No," said Race thickly. Paul had not moved. "Brot, you know we can't do that."

"No," said Stein. He kept his eyes on Mark. "It's up to you, Mark. Turn the station back to Brot or over to Race. Otherwise, I'm going back to Sector Headquarters to charge Brot with incompetence and ask to have him replaced. The way he's cut up they won't hesitate, particularly when they hear the wild things you're trying to do here. One way or another you've got to be stopped. You're playing games with ten thousand lives at this station."

"They've been informed at Sector," Mark said. "The daily reports have gone in on schedule ever since I landed."

"Don't talk like a colonist, Mark," said Stein. "You know I know how long it takes for anything from the daily reports to attract attention at the command level over at Sector.

They're more than half Navy there."

He dropped his hands from his shoulders.

"Last chance, Mark," he said.

He walked toward the door.

"My gun . . . give me . . . " husked Brot.

"No," said Mark. Stein disappeared through the bedroom door. "Paul you stay with Brot. Race—"

He looked at the assistant station master.

"I'm all right," said Race. His voice was clearer.

"If you're up to it, then, come along," said Mark.

"Mark—" Brot called huskily from the bed. *"Mark!"*

"Brot," said Race, "you know there's no other way. Make him lie back and rest, Paul. Give him a hypo if you have to. Go ahead, Mark. I'll witness."

Mark went out the bedroom door and across the living room, followed by the loose-jointed brown man. They went out the front door together and saw Stein perhaps sixty yards away from the building, heading toward a small airhopter. Race stopped, and Mark walked out from the Residence a half-dozen steps.

"Stein!" he called.

Stein turned, jerking out his side arm as he spun about. Mark was already diving toward the ground and drawing his own gun. A heavy fist struck him while he was still in midair, slamming him against the hard earth. Mist seemed to flood in around the blurring figure of Stein, and Mark felt the gun buck in his hand, as he got off at least a single shot . . .

He woke to a vision of whiteness that slowly resolved itself into the view of a ceiling. He felt exhausted to the point of strengthlessness, and the area of his left shoulder and chest was heavy and uncomfortable. He reached for it with his right hand and found himself thick with bandaging there.

He lowered his gaze, digging his chin into his chest to look level, and saw the foot of his bed and then Brot's hospital bed, with Brot sitting up in it, and Race, Paul, and Orv all standing about. All four men were watching him.

"Stein?" Mark asked, hearing his voice come out almost as husky as Brot's.

"Killed," said Race. "Through the neck. A clean shot."

Mark felt a sudden, unexpected surge of emptiness and self-hatred wash through him. All at once, reasonlessly, he remembered Stein and another outposter whose name he could not now remember taking turns carrying him about on their shoulders when he had been very young.

"I was aiming at his head," he said faintly.

"Clean shots both ways." Race's voice seemed to boom in his ears. "He got you from above on your way down—the slug went in just by your left shoulder blade, then down and out just above your left hipbone in front. No important organs holed on the way through. You'll be up in a week or so. I gave it my witness—a fair and private dispute."

"I was aiming at his head . . ." whispered

Mark. Whispering, he fell asleep.

He was up and around, as Race had predicted, in eight days, but he wore bandages for another two weeks. Meanwhile, Race had briefed the colonists on the changes that were taking place. Paul, who had been back at the Earth-City the most recently of any of them except Mark, had helped on the briefing.

The colonists had taken these sessions well. There was a minority—older people mainly, Paul told Mark—who were fearful of what was being planned and done. But most of the colonists had revealed a deep-lying hunger for change, any change, in their outcast situation. It was a little startling to Paul, even after six years on Post, to realize how the chance-dictated brutality of deportation from the Earth of their birth had rankled unchanged in some of the colonists for as much as three-quarters of a lifetime.

As for Mark, he found that something had happened to him as a result of the death of Stein. He had lived with his determination to deal with the Meda V.'Dan as long as he could remember. In all that time he had imagined all sorts of contingencies. But he had not imagined having to shoot Stein. Lying on his bed that first eight days, and later while walking around still bandaged, he faced the fact that, if necessary, he would do the same thing again. But in some hidden part of his inner self there was now scar tissue where there had formerly been life and sensitivity.

Luckily, he soon had other matters to think about. His bandages had barely come off for good when Jarl came searching for him, to take him back to the comptroller's building.

The building was now reroofed, walled, finished, and furnished. A large tank-type integrator, back to back with a wide chart table, took up the centre of the room. A few chairs and lesser calculators helped fill the remaining space between these two large items and the walls, which were hung with files of all types, from microspool through image cubes to chart and graph. Just at the moment, a clutter of papers and books hid the surface of the chart table, and on top of these were a number of small objects of straw, wood, or native stone. It was to these that Jarl directed Mark's attention.

"There's your answer," Jarl said. "Native handiwork."

Mark picked up the nearest object, which was the crudely carved wooded figure of a man sitting on a stump and sharpening an axe. Mark turned it over in his hand, examining it from different angles, and then put it down again.

"Answer to what?" Mark asked.

"You wanted something to trade to the Meda V'Dan," Jarl said. The big man was surprisingly enthusiastic. "It's not only the ideal sort of trade stuff for us, it's the only thing we can afford to trade. I tore this colony apart economically—past, present, and future, right down to every nail in every building and every potato in every potato field. It can't afford to trade its old shoes, if it comes down to doing business in hard goods, the kind of thing the Meda V'Dan raid Outpost Stations for, according to your records. All the light and heavy machinery, the instruments, the agricultural and industrial chemicals—trade any of that and we'll be in trouble. We not only don't have any to spare, we don't have enough for ourselves right now. But"— he gestured to the objects on the table—"this stuff!"

"What makes this so good?" Mark asked.

Jarl looked at him curiously. "You really don't know?"

"I've got an idea," said Mark. "But you're the one who has to sell me on whatever notion you've come up with. So tell me why."

"Well, look at it!" said Jarl. "All of it together hasn't got the value of a credit dollar. In short, it costs us nothing in real terms. Only the time and labour of the colonists who carve or build or weave it. But we can trade it to the Meda V'Dan for the same things we're short of."

"Why?"

"Why?" Jarl stared at him.

"If there's no real value in it, why would the Meda V'Dan want it?"

"Because there's an unreal value in it—an art value!" Jarl said. "The Meda V'Dan may not have any use for it themselves, judging by the way the records say they've reacted as individuals visiting the Earth-City, when they were introduced to human art back there. But they can turn around and trade these things off again at a profit to the Unknown Races farther in toward the galaxy's centre!''

"And what makes you think that any of the Unknown Races would want these things?"

"Because somewhere in there, there's a race which appreciates art and deals in it!" said Jarl impatiently. "You've seen the sort of little gadgets the Meda V'Dan give as gifts to the brass at Navy Base. Stuff like that sparkle-cube, or whatever it was, Ulla had around her neck on the ship coming out here. Every time the Meda V'Dan have actually traded with the Colonies, they've traded the things the outposters or the Navy asked for— tools, instruments, metals, practical things. When they raid Outpost Stations that's the sort of thing they take. But when they give gifts, they give trinkets like Ulla's cube. Don't you see? They don't make the trinkets, or they'd be using them as a trade stuff with us. But they know some race that does, maybe several races. So they deal in *their* trinkets, and they'll deal in ours. Down toward Galactic Centre there are bound to be aliens as interested in our native handiwork as we are in theirs."

He stopped talking at last, and stood watching Mark, waiting for him to answer. But Mark looked again at the handiwork on the chart table before speaking.

"Maybe," he said, after a moment.

Temper flared in the big man's eyes.

"Maybe!" Jarl echoed. "Here I turn this colony's assets inside out for you and come up with something out of nothing that's damn near a miracle—"

"I said maybe." Mark cut him short. "Nine out of ten guesses about the Meda V'Dan have been wrong from the start, usually because whoever was guessing couldn't help assuming human reactions in alien minds. Maybe this is a wrong guess, too. All right, we'll try it out on the Meda V'Dan, but I'll believe it's working when I see it actually happening. Not before."

He went off, leaving Jarl fuming. But once outside the comptroller's building, he turned to hunt up Lily Betaugh. He found her in the underground records room with one of the three assistants—the sociologist—that she had so far chosen to help her. Mark took her aside to tell her privately about Jarl's idea.

"What do you think of it from what you've been able to put together about the Meda V'Dan so far?" Mark asked.

"I haven't put together much of anything yet," said Lily. "What you asked me to do isn't something anyone can come up with overnight, or something I'd be sure enough about to announce without a lot of checking."

"All right," said Mark. "Then give me your opinion without being sure. What's your guess about the Meda V'Dan trading for our handiwork?"

She hesitated.

"There are indications they do a lot of trading," she said, after a second. "And of course the more they trade, the more likely they'd be to trade in all sorts of different things."

He looked at her for a moment, thoughtfully.

"I think," he said at last, "the academic outlook you had back at Belgrade is slowing you down too much. This isn't a scholarly research project where you can take as many years as you want to work up conclusions. I want guesswork I can act on tomorrow—if not today. So suppose you forget everything else for a minute and give me the picture of the Meda V'Dan as you see them, now, without having all the evidence you'd like to consider."

Still, she hesitated.

"If you can't do this," he said, and heard a hardness of threat in his own voice that, unreasonably, started him thinking about Stein again, "you're no use to me here."

She lifted her small face to him.

"If I have to," she said, "all right, then. The Meda V'Dan claim to look on us as primitive compared to them. They look down their noses at us. If they were humans, there'd be some reason to think that such an attitude was at least in part compensatory, and so not entirely justified. But they're not human and maybe this is a case where the human rule doesn't work. We know they're not very interested in spending any time at our Earth-City —even though a number of them have visited it with red-carpet treatment—and they definitely don't want any humans cluttering up their own world, or worlds. Also, they evidently can get along with a number of different races and cultures, since they trade with the Unknown Races as well as with us. But they seem to have no morals or ethics where their treatment of humans is concerned—witness their frequent raids on these Outpost Stations, which their spokesmen immediately disavow. On the other hand, in order to survive as a civilization, they must have some internal rules system of their own. But no one seems to have any clue to what it is."

She broke off.

"Shall I go on?" she asked. "It's all like that. One bit of evidence almost contradicting another."

"No," Mark said. He was thoughtful again. "But get to work writing it up—as much as you can in the next three days—and I'll read it as I go."

She frowned up at him.

"Go where?"

"To talk to the Meda V'Dan themselves."

"You can't be serious—" she was beginning, but he was already on his way out.

He went to the Residence to announce the same intention to Race, who stared at him and reacted with words parallel to, if not identical with, Lily's.

"Go *now*?" asked Race.

"Why not?" said Mark. "Spal tells me he's got his Wild Bunch crews ready to lift and gun a couple of the scout ships, and Maura Vols can navigate for both ships if we stay close together. Meanwhile her students can learn by doing."

"But," said Race, "when they hear about this at Sector—" He looked out a window of the Residence at the green fields and the darker green of variform oak trees beyond. "The summer's going fast and I don't want to have to fight Meda V'Dan and winter weather at the same time. We'll get started right away."

CHAPTER EIGHT

It was not a troublesome flight to the solar system under a GO star code-named K39, where the Meda V'Dan were known to have at least one inhabited world. It was only slow, as Maura Vols agonized over her decisions and insisted on checking and rechecking her work each time before they made a position shift— five of which were required to bring the two scout ships to the periphery of K39. Maura was proving unexpectedly stubborn about details. But she had shed her black wig and, in spite of this, looked fifteen years younger under the natural grey of her own hair. It was not an unusual transformation among the colonists as Mark knew. The rate of male die-off in a lottery shipment, once the Colonies were reached, was three times that of the female, and among the women who survived, several often showed evidence of such an apparently reasonless rejuvenation.

Within three minutes of accomplishing shift into position by the K39 system, however, they were challenged by Meda V'Dan ships.

"I'm the commander of Abruzzi Station Fourteen, Garnera Six," answered Mark in human speech as soon as the laser talk-light beam between his ship and the invisibly distant Meda V'Dan ship was stabilized. "Outposter Mark Ten Roos. I'm here to give your Most Important Person a chance to try and establish trading patterns with our independent colony."

There was a short silence at the other end. Then the loudspeaker before Mark rattled in the heavy-syllabled Meda V'Dan tongue.

"I don't like your attitude," said Mark. "I'll make a point of complaining about it to your Most Important Person when I talk to him. You don't seem to realize whom you're talking to. I suppose I can't blame you. You Meda V'Dan have never encountered humans from an independent colony before. If you know what's good for you, you'll take me to meet your Most Important Person without any more delay, and with a decent amount of courtesy from now on."

The talk-light beam was broken abruptly from the other end. A moment later, six Meda V'Dan ships, each one several times the size of the two scout ships Mark had brought, appeared around them. Two of the alien vessels flanked the scout ships, the other four clustered behind. All six Meda V'Dan ships began to move forward slowly.

"We're under escort," Mark said to the other scout ship over his intership circuit. "Start moving, and keep together."

They moved off as a unit, the alien ships guarding the smaller human vessels like a trout escorting minnows.

Turning from the screen, Mark caught sight of the face of Lily Betaugh staring up at him.

"You can't talk to the Meda V'Dan like that," Lily whispered, glancing around to see that none of the others in the scout ship command cabin was close enough to overhear. "It's just asking for trouble."

He looked back down at her, a little grimly.

"Don't anthropomorphize," he answered. "They've got no way of knowing how important I am. All they know about human rank and authority is what other humans have told them—at the Navy Base and back at the Earth-City. But the Meda V'Dan themselves don't tell the truth except when it suits them. How do they know the other humans told them everything—and told it right?"

She stood for a moment. Then she shook her head.

"It's still an awful risk," she said.

"Maybe," said Mark. "But something that needs to be done has risk in it. And there's something you ought to keep in mind. They really don't know us any better than we know them, so anything's possible on both sides. Will you go ask Paul Trygve to join me up here from the rear gun post?"

Lily went. A few minutes later, Paul showed up in the command room. He was the only other outposter Mark had brought along.

"Paul," said Mark, pointing at the map screen, "they're taking us into the fourth planet of the system, just as we figured. When we land, I want to leave nearly everyone aboard but you, Lily, Spal, and me. We'll make up a VIP committee to go in and talk to the Meda V'Dan in person."

"All right," said Paul, but he hesitated. "You're sure you don't want to leave at least one outposter with these two boat-loads of colonists?"

"No. I may need you," said Mark. "Anyway, they might as well start now learning to get along on their own without an outposter to fall back on."

The escorting alien ships brought the human vessels into a fused-rock landing area just outside what Mark judged to be a city in the planet's northern hemisphere. Viewed on the scout ship screens during landing, the buildings were remarkably uniform and regularly spaced. They were windowless, dome-roofed towers of something like ten stories in height, rising out of what looked almost like a vast metal platform some five miles square and a hundred and fifty feet thick, its edges sloping down to fused rock all around. Altogether, the appearance was more that of some monster machine than of an inhabited city.

Once they had landed, there was no further Meda V'Dan activity about the two human ships for nearly four hours. At the end of that time, a talk-light beam pinged upon the outer hull of the two vessels and an alien voice speaking in Meda V'Dan invited the commander outposter to come forth and be conducted to a meeting with the authorities, to whom he could explain his presence.

Mark, Paul, Lily, and Spal left their scout ship and found a small, floating platform vehicle, pilotless, waiting for them beside the ship. Once they had all stepped up onto its flat metal bed, the vehicle began to move. It picked up speed as it headed toward the city, slid up the angle of the edge of the vast platform, keeping a constant distance from the sloping surface, and moved on in among the forest of windowless buildings.

It stopped at last by the base of one of these, and a door there slid downward out of sight to show a short interior passageway. Still, there were no Meda V'Dan to be seen.

"Come along," said Mark.

The four went into the building. The door closed behind them, and another opened at the end of the short passage. They walked forward and through this new door to find themselves on a narrow, fragile-looking metal catwalk that soared way ahead of them through girders and unlighted space until it was lost in gloom. The second door slid shut behind them, and a small glow appeared about the metal of the catwalk, illuminating their way.

Lily made a short noise in her throat, halfway between a choke and a sound of retching.

"Hang on," said Mark. "You'll get used to the smell after a bit. Don't hold your nose or anything like that. They may be watching —and remember, they don't think we smell like a bed of roses, either."

Still, Mark himself was tempted to hold his breath as he led the rest of them across the catwalk. The stink of the Meda V'Dan corridor was something like the smell of rancid animal fat, with a sweetish, unnatural over-taste that caught in the human throat and seemed to cling there.

Somewhere in the gloomy midair, their cat-walk intersected with another, angling in from the left. All routes in the intersection were blocked but the one leading off to the right. Mark turned that way, with the others following, and perhaps a hundred feet farther on they came to the open entrance of another short passageway.

This led to a white-coloured door that slid aside at their approach and let them into a wide room containing a very human-looking set of padded furniture. As the door closed behind them, a strong breeze began blowing from the walls, and, shortly, the native smell of the aliens began to diminish.

"They've had humans here before," said Paul.

"Bound to have had," said Mark, looking around the room. "Brass from Navy Base, if nothing else. Any time now—"

A startled grunt from Spal interrupted him. The ex-Marine had dropped down into one of the armchairs—to all appearances like any such piece of padded furniture made on Earth—and found it unyielding. What ap-peared to be spring-filled cushions covered with fabric was evidently only an imitation of such in some hard material.

Paul laughed, and reached down to put his hand to the nap of the carpet underfoot.

"Like wire," he said to Mark, straightening up. "Wouldn't surprise me if it was wire." He went across the room to a farther door, which slid aside as he approached. He glanced into the room beyond. "At least we've got sanitary facilities. Unless they're imitation, too."

He reached inside and turned a tap on what appeared to be an ordinary enough human-style washstand. Water spurted into the basin below. Paul turned the tap off, wrinkling his nose. He stepped back into the room as the door he had just leaned through closed once more behind him.

"Their water smells too," Paul said. He looked at Mark. "Now what? We just wait?"

Mark nodded.

This time the wait stretched out. Several times, Mark went back out through the obediently opening doors and back along the catwalk as far as the intersection. There he stood, listening. Occasionally, from far below there would be the faint, distant, shivering sound of metal striking against metal, or a noise like that of a heavy weight dragged over a concrete floor. When he went back to the room, his nose had become so accustomed to the thick Meda V'Dan odour that the clean air of the steadily ventilated room smelled flat and strange in his nostrils.

The fourth time he came back from such an excursion, his step was rapid and brisk.

"We've waited long enough," he said to Paul clearly and loudly as he came in. "Nearly six hours and we're here without food or drink. If no one's shown up by the time the six hours are up, we'll head back to the ship."

Less than ten minutes later, the door to the room opened of its own accord, and a smaller version of the floating platform vehicle that had brought them to the city entered the room. On its flat bed was a small stack of packages—Navy-issue food and drink in decay-proof containers.

Spal stepped hastily toward it, and Lily slid off the hard cushion of the imitation chair on which she had been curled up, with her legs folded under her. Mark put out a hand and stopped the ex-Marine.

"No," he said, his voice echoing a little from the walls in the silence. "I don't think so. We didn't come here to be fed issue rations. These Meda V'Dan have to be either pretty poor or pretty ignorant to offer refreshment like this to us."

The platform hovered where it was for a few seconds longer. Then it slowly backed out of the room and it was gone.

"But, Mark," said Lily. "I'm—" She broke off as Mark's gaze came around hard upon her. She sighed and climbed slowly back up on her chair. The other two men, watching Mark, said nothing.

After another dozen minutes, the door opened again. The platform floated back in, this time carrying several tall sealed bottles and four of the large silver packages that held a complete meal each for a stateroom-class passenger on a human spaceship.

"Better," said Mark.

Paul picked up the bottles one by one and looked at them.

"Rhine wine, brandy," he said, "and bottled water." He helped Spal transfer the platform's load to the room's only table. Once unloaded, the platform slid quietly out.

The rest ate and drank hungrily. Mark drank only some bottled water.

"You ought to eat," said Lily.

He shook his head, barely hearing her voice against the background of his thoughts, as he sat in one of the hard imitation chairs, a disposable cup of water in his hand. He was here at last among the homes of the Meda V'Dan after years of imagining how he would get here, and the reality of it had kindled a grim fire of exultation in him that was acting on his thoughts like an explosive stimulant. Ideas raced one another through his mind. He had to fight back the impulse to get up and pace the floor under the fever they roused in him.

The door to the room slid open.

They all looked up, and Mark got to his feet as a Meda V'Dan rode into the room on a small platform vehicle. Like all the aliens, to human eyes he seemed identical with every other Meda V'Dan Mark had seen. His loose shirt was white with swirled black patterns, and his black and white checkered pants were stuffed into high red boots, each of which had a chain of what seemed to be small, burning fires looped around each boot top.

"Ou'posser Com'der Mar' T'Roos," he said awkwardly in human speech, staring impartially at them all, "ozzer Lords and Cap'ins. Welcome."

"Thanks," said Mark, and the eyes of the alien swung around to focus on him for just a second before slipping aside to stare past his right shoulder. "Who've we got to thank for all of this?"

The Meda V'Dan fell back into his own tongue.

[May thank me, human,] he said. [In rightness all call me Lord and Greatest Captain He of Fifty Names. Graciously I yield to importunities of humans clamouring to petition Most Important Person of the Meda V'Dan.]

His gaze shifted from Mark for a moment to flicker over the small figure of Lily, then return to station off Mark's shoulder.

[Not usual,] he said, [humans bearing their young among us of the Meda V'Dan. Nor are we sure are alien whelps welcome here.]

"You're talking about an adult," replied Mark. "This lady is an independent colonist named Lily Betaugh. And she's not only grown up, she's a woman of wisdom—of philosophy."

"Phil'sss . . . " Attempting to imitate Mark's pronunciation of the human word, He of Fifty Names failed utterly. In Meda V'Dan, he added, [The sound is not known to me.]

"Philosophy," said Mark. "That which a people believe to be true about themselves and their relation to the universe."

[Ah, philosophy.] Fifty Names came up with a word Mark had not learned in the Meda V'Dan vocabulary.

"Is that it?" Mark said. "All right. She's a student and teacher of philosophy of the Meda V'Dan."

[That is easily told,] said Fifty Names. [The Meda V'Dan were old and rich when all other races were unborn and unconceived. The

Meda V'Dan shall be rich and unchanged when all other races have died. For only we know the secret of the universe and will live forever, as we have already lived forever. Therefore, it is in the Meda V'Dan alone that we of the Meda V'Dan believe, and that is our philosophy. All else is supposition and error, that in which barbaric and short-lived races believe.]

"I see," said Mark.

[Good that you see,] said Fifty Names. [But there becomes in me an impatience. You have come searching out the Most Important Person of the Meda V'Dan for talk. Talk, then.]

"I intend to," said Mark.

But having said that much, he said no more. For a long moment the silence grew in the room, then Fifty Names himself broke it.

[Human speech speaks of speaking but speaks no speech,] he said. His words played on the active Meda V'Dan term for dialogue between alien and human and were either a joke or a sneer.

"That's because I'm still waiting for the Most Important Person to arrive," said Mark.

[I am here.]

"You're here," said Mark. "He isn't."

[To humans I am the Most Important Person.]

"Not to me, you're not," said Mark.

[Frail human with little ships, do you try to insult a Lord and Greatest Captain of the Meda V'Dan?]

"As Outposter Commander of the Independent Colony of Abruzzi Station Fourteen on

Garnera Six," said Mark, "I'm insulted to be kept waiting by a Meda V'Dan of lesser rank than should be talking to me. In fact, I'm just about out of patience. I told the Meda V'Dan on the ships that intercepted us that they evidently didn't realize whom they were talking to. Evidently you don't know either. We'll be leaving."

He turned to the other three humans.

"Let's go," he said, and walked toward the door, which opened before him.

[Humans will leave when given leave, not otherwise.] The alien voice followed him.

"We'll leave when I say so," said Mark, still walking toward the door. "Interfere with us in any way, and the Meda V'Dan will never deal with another human being again."

He was at the door.

[Pause,] said Fifty Names. [There may be a misconception here.]

Mark stopped at the doorway and turned about, to look back at the Meda V'Dan. He did not come back into the room, however, and after a second, Fifty Names stepped down from the platform.

[A misconception,] he said, [may exist.]

"Not on my part," said Mark.

[The possibility exists that I have been wrongly informed by the Lords and Great Captains of the ships which met you as you came close to our sun,] Fifty Names said. [If this is so, they are criminals and no better, and they will be punished for this as soon as they can be identified and apprehended. Unfortunately, they have all left this solar sys-

tem on business of their own before I was told
you were waiting here. But if we can find
them, they will suffer—]

"Never mind," said Mark. He was still
standing in the doorway. "I'm not interested
in unimportant individuals, but in your Most
Important Person. If I can't see him shortly,
we're leaving."

[You will see him.]

Mark turned and came back into the room.

"Sit down again," he told the other three,
then turned his attention back to Fifty Names.
"How soon?"

[It is impossible to tell—wait,] said Fifty
Names, as Mark turned once more toward the
door, [but perhaps an hour of meeting can be
found and established. Not precisely—]

"It'll have to be precisely," said Mark.

[Possibly, possibly it can be precisely deter-
mined.]

"And it'll have to be soon. We've waited
longer than we should already."

[Soon,] said Fifty Names. [As soon as possible.]

"Now," said Mark.

[That is not possible.]

"Then," said Mark, "we're leaving now."

[If you leave, you leave,] said Fifty Names.
[Now is not possible. Not even in a little while
is it possible. Not even if He of Most Importance wished it, would it be possible in any
case other than an emergency for all Meda
V'Dan. He is our Most Important Person and
his duties are many.]

"In six more hours, then—at the outside,"

said Mark.

[Impossible. Three days at the least.]

"I'll make that eight hours," said Mark. "But we're not staying here any three days."

[Possibly, just barely possibly, he might speak to you, if all things go well, in under two days.]

"No," said Mark. "Eight hours. All right, ten hours. But at the end of ten hours we lift our ships."

[I tell you, human—and I am a Lord and Greatest Captain among the Meda V'Dan—he whom you wish to speak to is not merely of this universe but in part of another. He is not to be summoned in a moment to an unknown meeting. If I died for it, he could not be spoken to by you in under sixteen hours.]

"Ten," said Mark.

[Sixteen,] said Fifty Names. [Go if you wish.]

"We'll wait ten, then leave," said Mark.

[Very well. I will try to bring you to him in less than sixteen. But I promise nothing and expect nothing. Nor should you.]

Fifty Names stepped back up on the platform vehicle, and it carried him out. The door closed behind him.

"Sixteen hours," said Paul, looking after the alien. "Maybe we should go back to the ship."

"No," said Mark. He looked around the room and spoke to the walls. "We'll need bedding. Blankets. And some way of controlling this lighting so that we can darken the room for sleeping."

In less than twenty minutes, the platform

vehicle returned with a neat stack of white
Navy blankets and two small, brown pillows.
A panel opened in the wall to the left of the
door, revealing a rheostatlike control knob,
and Mark, experimenting, found that it was
possible to dial the illumination about them
from darkness up into a brilliance that made
them shield their eyes. He turned the control
back down until the room was in a dimness
only slightly brighter than that of the gloom
about the catwalk outside.

There were enough blankets so that they
could make pads to protect themselves from
the stiff fibres of the imitation rug and still
have a blanket apiece left for wrapping themselves. When they were all rolled up in their
blankets but Mark, Mark turned the lights
down into total darkness and then felt his way
back along the wall to his own pad and
blanket.

He was busy there for some while, then he
felt his way across to where memory told him
Spal was lying. The ex-Marine woke at the
touch of an exploring hand on his face.

"What—" Spal began. Mark put his hand
over the other's mouth, choking off his voice.

"Quiet." Mark breathed in the short man's
ear. "Listen now, and don't talk. Hang on to
your covering blanket, but climb up on my
shoulders when I get to my feet. Once you're
up, wrap the blanket around you so it hides
me completely. Got that?"

Mark removed his hand from Spal's mouth.

He obeyed. It was slow and clumsy in the
darkness, but in a couple of minutes, Spal was

riding Mark's shoulders and the blanket the ex-Marine had wrapped around his shoulders cloaked Mark from view.

Once Mark felt the blanket around him and the smaller man firmly on his shoulders, he started to work his way by memory back to the wall, and then along the wall to the light control. He almost missed it, but feeling the edge of the door sent him back with surer aim. A moment later he had it. He turned the light up until it was barely possible to see Spal's now-empty pad, the two blanket-wrapped forms of Lily and Paul, and a blanketed shape huddled against the wall where Mark's own sleeping position had been.

Mark turned, balancing the weight of Spal on his shoulders. Peering out through a crack where he held the two edges of blanket together before him, he headed toward the small, blanket-wrapped figure of Lily. When he got there, he saw that she was wide awake and watching him without moving.

"Get up," he whispered.

She tossed the edge of her blanket back and stood up—a slightly tousled doll-shape.

"Come on."

He turned, again carefully, and led the way toward the door of the room, which opened before them. Together, the three in the guise of two went down the corridor and out onto the walkway.

It was more than a slightly effortful distance to the intersection of the two walkways for Mark, carrying the weight of Spal. When Mark reached the intersection, he pressed up against the railing next to the barrier that closed off the intersecting walkway, and gradually squatted down under the blanket until Spal's feet touched the walkway floor on each side of him.

"Just stand here, both of you," Mark murmured from under the blanket. Easing out from beneath Spal's legs, he opened the blanket a crack. One of the barriers, and the dark stretch of barred-off walkway beyond, was inches from him. The barred-off walkway did not glow, and its shape seemed to vanish in the gloom less than a dozen feet from where he squatted.

"Stand here for fifteen minutes after I go," he whispered. "Then go back to the room and lie down. Come back out here three hours from now, and if I'm not here, wait for me. Did you get that?"

Spal grunted affirmatively, overhead. Clinging closely to the shadow of the barrier itself, Mark slipped out from under the skirt of Spal's blanket and through a small gap between the barrier and the railing into the darkness of the barred-off catwalk. He continued to crawl forward on his stomach down the dark catwalk floor until he had covered some distance. Then he paused and looked back.

Spal and Lily were twenty feet or more behind him, two disparate, blanket-wrapped shapes, staring out over the railing of their little catwalk at nothingness. Mark checked his wristwatch. The glowing hands stood at 1:17. He got to his feet and ran softly forward another fifty feet before he straightened up. Then he slowed to a rapid walk.

Slowly thereafter he came to a circular stairway, coiling downward. For a second he paused at the head of it, looking tensely in all directions about him. From below came the faint, distant, momentary sound of metal against metal.

Then he took hold of the railing of the stair and went down into darkness.

CHAPTER NINE

As he descended, he counted the steps. When he had reached the number of sixty-seven, his descending foot jarred on a different surface. Looking down and around, he saw that he had reached an intersection with another catwalk which soared off into the darkness on either side of him.

It was almost completely dark here—but not quite. A vague general illumination from somewhere prevented total obscurity, so that he was surrounded by a sort of heavy twilight. Farther below, there was an additional, vague glow of illumination, but either the atmosphere was naturally misty or the lower light was baffled in some fashion, because he could not see much beyond thirty feet in any direction. His nose was all but numb to the Meda V'Dan odour now, but it seemed to Mark that here the air felt thicker in his lungs than it had been above.

He continued downward. Another sixty-seven steps of descent brought him to a second catwalk. He paused and calculated. The steps were nearly eight inches apart. One hundred and thirty-four steps that far apart would place him one thousand and seventy-two inches, or roughly ninety feet below the level of his starting point, which was level with the entrance from the city platform through which they had entered the building earlier. He should now be, therefore, some ninety feet underground—if that term applied here—but still almost seventy feet above the level of the fused-rock area on which their scout ships had been escorted to a landing.

Obscurity still yawned below him, but the occasional sounds of heavy weights dragging on a coarse surface, or of metal shivering against metal, were much louder now. The stairs continued downward, and so did he.

But now, as he descended, the illumination from below grew stronger, and gradually he began to make out shapes in the darkness below him. These grew from vague outlines to reveal themselves as tall stacks of various objects, like crates and materials in a warehouse, and with the last of another set of sixty-seven descending steps he set foot finally on a solid floor, surrounded by high piles of things.

The floor was metallic, and his first step onto it rang more hollowly than his next as he moved away from the stairs. He looked back to examine the foot of the staircase and saw that below the bottom tread was what seemed to be something like a trapdoor with a circular handle. Presumably the staircase continued on down. He took hold of the handle and tried to lift the door, but it was either locked or too heavy for his strength. He gave up the effort and turned away to examine the nearest stack of objects.

These turned out to be a set of oblong shapes about the size and general appearance of coffins. But when he reached out to lift one from the top of a stack, it nearly floated into the air at his touch. The objects, whatever they were, were almost as light as air-filled balloons. But he could find no seam or crack in them to suggest that they might be opened, and their use as objects in themselves was unguessable.

He moved on, finding each stack made up of different cases or objects and equally incomprehensible, until he came unexpectedly upon a small pile of the same white Navy-issue blankets that had been provided above for their bedding. As he was making a rough estimate of how many blankets there might be in the pile, there was the shivering sound of metal on metal right behind him.

Turning sharply, he was just in time to step back as one of the miniature platforms floated by him, either towing or being pushed by a low, treaded vehicle with what seemed to be a number of long, jointed, grasping arms sprouting from its top surface. The platform was already carrying several small objects, and as it passed, one of the jointed arms from the treaded vehicle picked something more from a stack opposite the pile of blankets.

Then both platform and treaded vehicle moved on.

Mark followed them. Their pace was not slow, and he had to jog to keep up with them. Together, they collected and loaded on the platform several more objects before steering away among the stacks to come up against the wide, soaring surface of a wall in front of which some sort of conveyor lift-belt was in continuous upward motion.

The burden of the platform was transferred to the steadily upward-moving arms of the conveyor lift, and the two automated vehicles moved off. Mark stepped closer to examine the lift.

Like the staircase, it too went down through the floor of this warehouse area in which he stood. But here there was an opening through which the belt and arms rose. Mark got as close to the belt as he could and gazed downward.

He stared into a vast, brightly lighted area equal in size to the warehouse floor on which he stood and possibly a hundred feet deep within its massive circular wall. Half a dozen incredibly massive, metal shapes were held in the midspace of this chamber by massive girders. The appearance of these metal shapes was unfamiliar, but everything about them, the strength of the girders supporting them as well as the thickness of the obvious power leads leading from their lower ends into the floor beneath them, identified them as power source engines. But where was the machinery that required such power? Nothing anywhere else in the building had signaled the presence of such machinery.

Mark looked at his watch. Incredibly, the hands stood at two minutes to four. The three hours he had mentioned to Spal and Lily were almost up.

He looked about him. He was not lost with respect to his starting point, which had been the foot of the staircase, in spite of his round-about movements in pursuit of the platform and the loading vehicle. Part of memory train-ing at Outposter's Academy had been the en-visioned reference grid on which, in unfamil-iar territory, a graduate automatically counted his steps and turns by mnemonic device. Standing by the conveyor now, he summoned up the grid image in his mind and ran mentally through the chart of numbered steps and turns he had taken since leaving the ladder's foot.

Envisioned, his path built itself as a white line by jogs and turns and loops from centre point A1 to an ending at square MNP93. The direct line between those two points would lay out a route of two hundred and eighteen feet at twenty degrees inclination to the base line of the wall now at his back.

There was no doubt he could find his way back to the staircase. But in routing himself around the stacked materials, he would take time, and then there would be the slow, hard climb up two hundred and one eight-inch steps to where Spal and Lily waited. At a rough estimate he would be close to forty minutes overdue by the time he reached them, and he did not have confidence in the level-headedness of either one of them that would ensure their not becoming impatient and doing something foolish that would attract the attention of the audio and probably visual monitors the Meda V'Dan obviously had on their human guests.

Mark looked at the steadily rising arms of the conveyor belt. Then he turned about and caught hold of a rising arm, stepping with both feet onto the one below.

The belt carried him upward. In a moment, the scene of the warehouse section floor was lost in obscurity once more below him. He was enclosed in grey twilight, moving up through nothingness beside an endless wall-surface that vanished in the darkness above, below, and on both sides of him.

The ride seemed to go on an interminable time. He glanced at his watch, at the glowing second hand sweeping its dial, and it seemed to him that the hand was moving very slowly.

Then there was a glimmer of light—a small spot of yellowish illumination directly above him. He approached it rapidly, and it grew in brightness until he saw it as a manhole-shaped opening in a darkly solid floor above, through which the conveyor belt was carrying him.

He crouched down, tensing himself for quick action in the face of whatever he might find in the light above.

The conveyor belt lifted him through. He had a glimpse of a reasonably lighted room as he leaped clear of the belt and landed, ready, with his back to the wall. But there was no one in the room, only a floating platform and a loader standing motionlessly by. Mark breathed deeply. Whatever activated the automated vehicles, it was not simply a matter of weight on the conveyor belt.

He straightened up and took a closer look at the room. It was almost more a passage than a room—long and narrow, reaching to a white-painted door at the far end. Toward the door end was either a small window or a vision screen pickup. He went toward it.

It was a vision screen, all right, with a control knob below it. Currently, it showed only darkness, and from somewhere about or behind it, an audio pickup brought him the sound of someone, undoubtedly human, breathing slowly and deeply, just on the verge of snoring.

He reached out and turned the knob. The darkness gave way to the view of a short, empty passageway leading to a green door. He turned the knob again and saw the end of a lighted catwalk leading from a door. He continued to turn the knob and the view moved along the catwalk until it reached an intersection with an unlighted catwalk, where two figures, one large, one small, wrapped in white blankets, stood waiting. This, then, was the observation room from which his actions and those of the others had been watched earlier by the Meda V'Dan. But there was no alien on watch now. Mark's subterfuge with the blanket, Spal, and Lily to hide his leaving of their common room had been unnecessary.

Mark shrugged. Alien psychology and reactions were unguessable. He turned the screen back to its view of the dark room and turned toward the door at his left. It slid open, revealing what was apparently a section of blank wall. But this, too, slipped aside, and he stepped through into the same corridor he had been viewing a second before on the screen.

He turned about in time to see the wall section close behind him once more. Closed, it looked as immovable as any other wall part in the passage. He turned and walked openly out onto the dark catwalk and along it until he came up behind Spal and Lily.

"Time to get back to sleep," he said.

Lily gasped. Spal did not start, but he turned about with a swiftness that was surprising.

"Mark!" Lily said. "How—"

"We won't talk here," he said, interrupting her. "Come on, both of you."

He led the way back to the room, and paused inside to dial the lighting up to the minimum level of illumination necessary for them to find their way back to their blanket pads on the floor. As he reached his own corner, Mark looked over at Paul. Paul lay breathing the calm, heavy breaths Mark had heard over the audio pickup connected with the vision screen, but his eyes were open and steady with question.

Mark shook his head imperceptibly, shook out the blanket he had bunched up to make it seem that he was still on the pad beneath, and settled himself seriously for sleep.

And in remarkably short time, actual sleep found him.

He woke with a start to the sudden glare of light in his eyes and the sight of Fifty Names —or at any rate, some Meda V'Dan wearing the same black and white shirt that Fifty Names had worn when Mark had last seen him—standing over them. Mark came to his feet by reflex, swiftly followed by Paul, and more slowly by Spal and Lily.

[By fortunate and unusual chance,] said Fifty Names, [He of Most Importance will face you briefly now.]

"We'll be right with you," Mark said. "It'll take us perhaps five minutes to get ready. Wait outside—and turn off your sight and sound surveillances of this room."

[Now is now,] said Fifty Names. [There is not time to wait.]

"Meda V'Dan," said Mark. "We'll come when we're ready—in five minutes or not at all. Wait outside and turn off your surveillance."

[If He of Most Importance knew of this, I could not do it,] said Fifty Names. [At my own risk I give you the time you ask for.]

He turned and rode out on the platform on which he had entered.

"Only," said Mark, looking after him, "I'll bet they go right on watching and listening to us."

He stepped to the table holding the remains of last night's meal and poured himself a cup of the bottled water that remained.

"Now's your chance to freshen up if you

want to grab it," he said to the others. "And you'd better grab it. No telling when the next chance is coming. Lily first."

Lily went off into the adjoining lavatory room and the door closed behind her. The two men joined Mark at the table. Paul filled himself a cup of water. Spal reached out to close his fist on the brandy bottle, then hesitated, glancing at Mark. When Mark said nothing the ex-Marine put the bottle to his lips and swallowed three times.

They were sharing some of the rolls and butter left over from the package meals when Lily rejoined them. Mark nodded Paul toward the lavatory.

Five minutes later, they stepped through the door of the room to find Fifty Names waiting in the passageway. An extra, empty floating platform nuzzled one on which the Meda V'Dan himself stood.

[The Commander will ride with me,] Fifty Names said. [Others, on the second vehicle.]

Once aboard, the platforms skimmed through an opening that unexpectedly appeared in a wall of the passageway—opposite the section of the wall that had moved aside to let Mark back into the passage the night before. They found themselves in a long, curving passage, down which the platforms slid with increasing speed until they were forced to decelerate so as to stop before an opening in a vertical shaft.

One by one the platforms floated up the shaft to a higher level. Then followed a quick, dizzying trip through several intersecting pas-

sageways and short changes in level until they
floated at last through a final opening into an
enclosure the size of a large ballroom. At
opposite ends of this room were what looked
like two daises about fifteen feet square and
six feet high supplied with metal chairs with
harp-shaped backs and saddle-shaped seats.
The platforms floated to the nearest of these
daises.

[You will rest here, all of you,] said Fifty
Names. He waited until they had stepped up
onto the dais, then swept away on his platform to the dais at the opposite end of the
room, and stepped up to seat himself in one of
the metal chairs there.

Mark himself sat down and the others
followed his example. The metal chairs were
not as uncomfortable as they had looked at
first glance.

"Now what?" asked Paul.

"I guess we wait," said Mark, "after all."

But the wait was not long. Within a few
minutes, the wall behind the other dais slid
aside to reveal a Meda V'Dan wearing boots,
loose pants, and shirt all of pure white, without ornament or design of any kind upon him.
He took the chair beside Fifty Names and
stared across the perhaps eighty feet of distance at the humans.

There was a moment of silence and stillness. Then the walls of the room opened in a
dozen places, and several dozen Meda V'Dan
ran out, one of them carrying what looked like
a silver rod, pointed at both ends. Shouting,
the one with the rod tossed it to another, who

fended off the approach of a third and tossed the rod again. They ran back and forth in the space between the two daises, yelping, struggling for the rod, and throwing it to one another. Gradually, the struggles for the rod became more violent. Scratches from the pointed ends brought blood to the faces and hands of the players. Then, without warning, the activity ceased. The shouting stopped. In a moment the players had all returned within the walls and the walls themselves had closed up again.

Abruptly, the dais under Mark and the others began to move. It slid forward toward the other dais, which was also in movement now, approaching from the other end of the room. The two heavy-looking structures swept toward each other until they were no more than twenty feet apart, then stopped. Mark squinted a little at the face of the Meda V'Dan in white. They were not quite close enough for him to make out details in the other's features, and it struck him that, even if he had been able to read expressions on the face of a Meda V'Dan, the distance was just enough to prevent this also.

The Meda V'Dan in white turned his head toward Fifty Names and his lips moved. There was no sound to be heard on the human dais, but Fifty Names tilted his head as if listening, then straightened and looked across at Mark.

[He of Most Importance,] said Fifty Names, [says that your unfortunate circumstance is known to him. If the renegades who destroyed the station of your parents at your birth and

destroyed your parents also are ever discovered, they will be severely punished.]

"Thanks," said Mark dryly. "I take it, then,
that this search has been going on ever
since?"

[I am the voice of He of Most Importance,]
said Fifty Names. [It has been without cease.]

"I'm glad to hear it," said Mark. "But that
isn't what we came here to talk about."

Once more the head of He of Most Importance turned to Fifty Names and his lips
moved.

[I who am Most Important among the Meda
V'Dan know why you have come,] relayed the
voice of Fifty Names. [It is a happy moment to
see you here, amicably among us. The trade of
humans is always welcome to the Meda
V'Dan. But you need not have come just for
that. Already we were prepared to visit you at
Abruzzi Fourteen before long and trade for
tools and hardware much demanded of us by
other inferior races like yourselves.]

"It's not tools and hardware we're interested in trading," said Mark. He turned to
Spal. "Let's have the box."

Spal unhooked from his belt the small
leather box containing samples of colonist
handicraft Jarl had earlier shown to Mark.

"Put it on the platform, there. Better open it
too. They might not know how." Mark pointed
to the platform vehicle that had carried them
to the dais and still floated alongside it. Spal
rose from his chair and knelt down at the edge
of the dais to place the box gently on the platform, unlocked and opened.

The platform slid away with its load in the direction of the other dais, where Fifty Names picked it up, unpacked its three small artifacts from protective padding, and passed them one at a time into the long-fingered hands of the figure beside him. He of Most Importance examined them one by one as the platform floated back to the human dais.

"In the interest of setting up a new trade line with the Meda V'Dan," said Mark, "we're willing to trade the first shipment at a fraction of the price we'd have required from our own people back on the Earth-City. Five of your flame hand weapons for each work of art."

The fingers of Most Importance, holding up the small wooden carving of an elephant and turning it about to inspect it, halted for a fraction of a second at the sound of these words. Then, casually, the fingers began to turn the carving about again.

The procedure of inspection was repeated with each of the objects, and they were passed back into the hands of Fifty Names. Most Importance turned his head, and his lips moved.

[These are crude toys,] relayed the voice of Fifty Names. [A spaceship full of them would not be worth one flame hand weapon. They are of no interest to us of the Meda V'Dan.]

"Perhaps not to Meda V'Dan," said Mark. "But to a good many of the races farther in toward the centre of the galaxy with whom the Meda V'Dan trade, these rare art objects, each one hand-fashioned individually by one of our race, are priceless. I'm surprised to hear you answer like that. If you don't want to handle them, we'll send ships in to these other races and take the extra profit of the trading ourselves."

For a moment after that statement, Most Importance did not move. He continued to sit absolutely still, staring at Mark. Then slowly his head turned to Fifty Names, his lips moved.

[I have never heard of a human that talked so wildly,] said the voice of Fifty Names. [Your little ships would not be able to make the trip down-galaxy to where the inner races begin to be found. Nor would you know where to find them. Only the Meda V'Dan know the skills of trading with many different races, and we know it because we are eternal and have lived so long that no people are strange to us. You are young and ignorant. If you try to trade with the inner races, you will only die in trying.]

"Want to bet?" said Mark. He got to his feet. "Sorry we couldn't agree. Possibly later on, after we've set up trade with the Unknown Races, we'll share some of it with you Meda V'Dan for a commission."

He looked at the others, who had imitated him automatically and were also on their feet.

"Come along," he said, and stepped toward the edge of the dais above the platform.

[Wait,] said Fifty Names. [You are leaving now?]

Mark stopped, and looked toward Most Importance.

The lips of the white-clad Meda V'Dan moved.

[Stay,] echoed the voice of Fifty Names. [We who achieve the position of Most Importance among the Meda V'Dan are more sensitive than ordinary individuals. I sense your deep disappointment, and I share the sorrow I feel in you that have come this distance only to fail. In charity, we will take a token consignment of sixty-seven of these primitive objects and in return, that the name of our goodwill to trade continue to be known, we will give you a dozen of our used flame hand weapons.]

Mark stepped back to his chair and sat down again, motioning the other three to follow suit.

"Thanks for your attempted kindness," he said. "But we wouldn't want to take advantage of you if you really don't realize the worth of these art pieces. Also, of course, valuable as they are, we couldn't consider giving them up for less than the price I mentioned. But, perhaps, just to show our goodwill in turn, I could add three pieces for no price at all. Merely as gifts."

There was a small sound from the direction of Paul's chair—something very like the noise of a choked-off snort of laughter. Mark glanced grimly at the other outposter, then back at Most Importance.

[The Meda V'Dan, in their wealth and power,] answered the voice of Fifty Names, [give gifts, but scorn to receive them. Possibly, in recognition of your faith in these small things, the dozen hand weapons we offer could be new, rather than used . . . .]

The bargaining began in earnest.

CHAPTER TEN

"I'm sorry, Mark," said Paul, once they were safely back aboard their scout ship and both small vessels were back in space, "I didn't plan to laugh back there. But when you mentioned gifts, after what they've been doing with the Navy Base people, it got me. It wasn't so much what you said, it was watching those two Meda V'Dan have to sit there and take it with a straight face."

"That's all right," said Lily. "But can you be sure they'll stick to the price they agreed to if we meet them with the sixty-seven new pieces of handicraft?"

Mark nodded at three of the so-called flame weapons—actually nothing more than projectors of tiny incendiary slugs, but slugs capable of generating a heat explosion of close to a million degrees.

"They paid for the three samples," he answered. "And to get them to part with arms of any kind is a victory. There wouldn't have been any sort of trade if they hadn't decided at first glance they could make a profit on the pieces. Jarl was right."

A wave of exhaustion swept through him. He was suddenly weary with a dead weariness that turned even his victory into a drab accomplishment. He took a hard grip on his thoughts.

"I'm going to get all our reactions down on tape while they're fresh," he said. "Spal, Lily, I want to check out with you anything you saw or figured out about the Meda V'Dan from seeing them close up like this—"

He paused, and blinked to clear his vision. A pearly mist was beginning to obscure things around him, and his balance was suddenly unsure. He put out an arm to steady himself against a bulkhead . . . and the next thing he remembered, Paul was helping him into a chair in his cabin.

A hand appeared with a glass partly full of a dark liquid, holding it to his lips. Automatically he drank, and the fire of unmixed liquor seared his throat and gullet. He choked, sputtering and pushing the glass away.

"What the hell's this—"

"It's our own whiskey. Drink it," said Paul, holding the unfinished liquor to Mark's lips in spite of Mark's efforts to brush it away. "Then you can get some sleep."

Mark gave up and drank what was left in a single fiery and effortful gulp.

He sighed with relief, leaning back in his chair. The shock of the whiskey had burned his vision clear again. He saw the furnishings of his cabin and Paul standing over him, Spal over near the door.

"I'm all right," he said.

"Sure," said Paul. "Just out on your feet. Sit there a minute until that hits bottom, and then we'll be able to trust you not to think of something to do instead of sleeping."

"Don't worry about it," said Mark. "I know when I have to quit."

"Sure," said Paul. "How do you feel now?"

Mark considered himself. He felt no reaction from the whiskey at all, only a sense of pleasant lassitude that was beginning to nibble at him.

"Better," he said. "You're right. I need a few hours. Don't worry, I'll turn in."

"All right, then," said Paul. He went out, Spal with him. Mark continued to sit where he was, feeling the lassitude grow and spread comfortably within him. He ran his mind over the events in the Meda V'Dan city. Much of it would need thought and discussion. The interesting part was the great power units he had seen through the conveyor-belt lift hole in the floor of the warehouse section . . .

The door to his cabin clicked shut. He had not heard it open. He looked over to see Lily coming toward him, carrying in both hands a double-sized white coffee mug. She had changed from the ship's coveralls she had worn to visit the Meda V'Dan into a pink garment that looked like a pyjama-robe combination. It must have been something she had brought from Earth. Possibly, he thought a little fuzzily—the whiskey was, he recognized, beginning to take hold after all—she too had decided to turn in. She looked like a living Dresden miniature of a woman, carrying the large cup to him. She put it into his hands.

"What's this?" he asked. The cup was hot.

"Soup," she said. "You've got to eat something, sometime. Don't argue. Here, hold it." She let go of the cup and deftly climbed up to sit on the arm of his chair, then took the cup back again and held it to his lips. "Drink it."

He tasted the steaming liquid cautiously. But its temperature was bearable. It was a thick, meaty soup of some sort, and after the first swallow or two, he found he was ravenous.

"I can hold it myself," he said. He took the cup from her and drank in small mouthfuls.

"You're strange," she said. He could smell the hint of some light, flowery perfume, from her, and almost feel the warmth of her small body against his left arm and shoulder. A little fuzzy from the whiskey, he enjoyed it. "You're very strange. You drive yourself like somebody twice your age and with twice your responsibilities."

"Duties," he answered.

"Duties?"

He leaned against the back of his chair to ease the weight of his head on wobbly neck muscles.

"Duties," he said, hearing the word sound a little blurred on his tongue. "Everyone's got duties. Mine began a long time ago—a long, long time ago."

"To your parents," she said softly. Her small hand pushed back the dark hair that had fallen forward on his forehead.

"No," he said. "To a race of fools."

Her fingers rubbed soothingly across his forehead.

"They aren't all fools."

"No," he said, half lost in his own memories and thoughts. "If they were, I could let it all smash up and forget it. But there've been a few good people, like my father and mother . . . like Brot . . . and my duty's to them."

"And not to us colonists?"

"Colonists!" He growled. "Oh, nothing against you personally, Ulla—"

Her fingers stopped moving on his forehead.

"Who?" she asked.

"Lily," he said. "Lily. Got mixed up, with all those *l*'s. Women with *l*'s in their names. Anyway, the point is it's not just colonists. There were two thousand colonists watching the night the Meda V'Dan burned our station and killed my parents, and not one of them did a thing. Against maybe fifty of the aliens."

"What could they have done?" Her fingers were again moving rhythmically back and forth across his forehead.

"Anything," he said, "but nothing. That's why it's not just my parents. It's not just the outposters or the colonists, it's all of them. The whole race of damn fools—and nobody to save them from their own mess but me."

He twisted his head a little awkwardly to look up into her face. Somehow, while he had been talking, she had slid off the arm of the chair until she lay with the light weight of her body pressing against him. He was suddenly conscious of the womanness of it. He tried to focus on her face, but she was too close. All that he could bring into focus were her two blue eyes, which were watching him solemnly from inches away.

"Lily . . ." He reached across with his right hand to lift her back up onto the arm of the chair, but at the touch of his hand, the thing she was wearing fell open down the front as if it had never been fastened, and the naked skin of his wrist and forearm pressed against her skin.

The contact was like an explosion in him—an explosion of everything in him that was young and had been long under pressure. But then, even in the second in which he picked her up and got to his feet, the tidal wave of all he had worked and lived with as long as he could remember came pouring back into that area the explosion had temporarily blasted empty.

He looked down at her savagely, thinking how easy it would be to give in now—to the first small break in his purpose that would lead to further cracking and final disintegration. From here he could slip back into the captured mass of humanity, accept the letters waiting for him on the community chain, and sink out of sight among the rest of those helpless in the grip of their historic time. He could, but he would not, and for a moment he stood feeling the bitterness of his purpose and equal bitterness at what it denied him.

He put her gently on her feet on the ground,

and automatically she gathered her clothing about her. Her face was pale now.

"I'm human," she said.

Fury boiled up in him.

"I'm not!" he said. "What's the matter with you? Don't you know what you are?"

She twitched as if he had hit her. Her eyes closed.

"I know," she whispered. "A midget . . . a freak."

"What?" he snapped at her. "What're you talking about? You're a colonist—that's what you are. Do you think I can be different with one colonist from what I am with the others? If I am, the whole thing breaks down."

His voice lowered on the last words.

"Get out of here," he said grimly. "I've got to get some sleep."

The colour had come back into her face. She smiled at him, and her eyes were almost luminous.

"Yes," she said softly, "you sleep now." She backed to the entrance of his cabin and then she was gone.

He stood looking at the door that had closed behind her. The adrenalin of his explosion had all drained away now. His head was no longer fuzzy from the whiskey, but he felt numb all over, heavy as a dead man in all his body and limbs. He turned, sat down on the side of his bunk, and pulled off his boots. Falling back on the bunk, he pulled its single cover up over him and fell asleep instantly.

He woke from heavy, prolonged slumber just as the scout ships were setting down from orbit around Garnera VI. There was no time to debrief Lily or Spal now on what they might have learned respectively about the Meda D'Van philosophy or military potential during the visit just past. He went out and took command of the ships during the landing.

There was a Navy courier ship—not much smaller than one of the heavy scout ships— already on the field before the station when they landed. Mark glanced at it briefly as the jar of landing went through the vessel he was in, but his mind was elsewhere now. He put in a call to the Residence building before leaving the scout ship.

Race's lean brown face appeared in the screen.

"Go well, Mark?" he asked.

"I think so," Mark said. "Want to get all the outposters—and Jarl, too, come to think of it —in the conference room at the Residence? I'll be there in a few minutes."

"They're already here," Race said.

"Fine. How's Brot?"

"Better," Race said. "He'll be there, too."

"Good." Mark broke the connection.

By the time he left the scout ship, Paul and the others had already gone, but an empty ground car had been waiting for him. He got in it and drove up to the Residence.

When he stepped at last into the conference room with its ring-shaped table, he found there not only the other outposters and Jarl Rakkal, but Ulla Showell. When she saw him, she got quickly to her feet from the chair where she had been sitting next to Jarl.

"Excuse me," she said. "I'll step out. I just dropped in on your station to see how Jarl was doing."

He looked at her grimly.

"You chose a bad time for it," he said.

Her face tightened.

"A bad time?" she echoed. "Why?"

"Because the Meda V'Dan will be hitting this section in about three days, unless I'm badly mistaken," he replied. He looked about the room at the faces of the others as they reacted to his words. "That means we haven't much time to get ready to fight them off."

CHAPTER ELEVEN

There was no sound or movement in the room. They were all looking at him.

"Mark," said Paul, after a moment, "are you sure? I mean you didn't mention anything about this—"

"I meant to as soon as we were back aboard," said Mark. "But it seems I ended up taking a small nap and not having the chance."

He turned to look directly at Ulla, who stared back at him, then started as if just wakened from an involuntary trance.

"Excuse me," she said again. She crossed the room and went out.

"But what makes you think they'd attack?" Paul said as the door closed behind her.

"I made the trip deliberately to stir them into doing just that—among other reasons for going," said Mark. "And I'm pretty sure the trip did it. Let's sit down."

They moved to the circular table and took seats around its outer rim. Brot, now in a mobile power chair, was slid into the gap in the ring shape that gave access to the open space in its centre.

"Paul," said Mark, when they were all seated, "have you had a chance to tell them about the trip itself?"

"I covered the gist of it," said Paul.

"All right, then I won't waste time doing the same thing," Mark said. He looked around at the other faces. "We got safely into the Meda V'Dan space area and city and out again because the aliens couldn't be sure of whether we were putting on an act or not. I behaved as if we had authority and importance, and the fact we showed up in a couple of Navy-type vessels but without any uniforms on our leaders made them cautious about calling any bluff I might be making. Then, it turned out we really had something they could use in trade—"

He broke off, looking at the big colonist.

"Thanks to Jarl, here."

"Thanks to you for saying so," said Jarl.

The hard voice of Brot broke in.

"But why should they hit us, Mark?"

"Because there's no point in their trading for those pieces of artwork we offered them if they can just take them," said Mark. "And also, because they don't like being bluffed any more than we do. One of the reasons I crowded them into talking business with us as soon as possible was because we were working against a time limit. The minute we showed up there, the way we did, they must have sent at least one ship to Navy Base to find out what the Navy knew about us. They were bound to come up with the information that the Navy had leased us the scout ships, and that'd be proof enough we didn't have any space-going fleet of our own. Their next move is obvious—hit us and settle the matter, as well as maybe wind up with a valuable haul."

"And you're telling us you deliberately provoked the Meda V'Dan into something like this?" Race demanded.

"That's right, Race." Mark looked across the curve of the table at the other man. "Because I wanted a chance to burn them; and teach them the lesson that it's a bad idea to raid Garnera Six Abruzzi Fourteen station. When they come, we're going to be ready for them. I took only two ships to visit them, deliberately, and we'll have two ships standing in the field. The other two we'll crew and lay off, armed and waiting just below the horizon. We'll set up an orbit watch, to give us a warning of their coming, and we'll evacuate the station itself. Also we'll set up gun posts in the woods around the station—anywhere there's cover—and that'll include use of the four fixed plasma rifles that are now on the two ships we'll leave in the field for them to see. We'll take them off and dummy up some kind of imitation rifles to mount in their place."

He looked over at Orval Belothen.

"You can raise us some kind of crew out of the village factories to do that for us, can't you, Orval?"

The round-faced outposter nodded. "There's a good new colonist in the furniture factory named Age Hammerschold," Orval said. "He can probably cut you wood imitation plasma rifles that'd fool anyone at fifty feet with a little paint. That is, if there's time enough, and I can get him to work steadily. He's a little unadapted yet. Mutters to himself and sits around a lot."

"All right," said Mark. "Then let's get down to details on the rest of it."

They spent the next five hours talking over plans. It was not until after dinner that Mark could find time to get together with Brot and Spal. They met in the small building at the station built by Mark to hold the station weapons and a small tool shop for their repair and maintenance.

"What did you learn about the Meda V'Dan we could use—if anything?" Mark asked the ex-Marine bluntly.

Spal shook his round head.

"Not much," he said. "In fact, not really anything. You know they didn't take us where we could see anything military."

"I told you beforehand," said Mark, "they wouldn't do anything like that. I asked you to use your eyes, anyway, and see if you couldn't figure out anything from what you did see."

"I know," said Spal. "I tried. But there's not much you can tell from what they showed us. In fact, nothing, really."

Mark looked at him for a moment.

"Spal," he said, "I brought you to this station and gave you this job, which is a lot better job than you'd have got if you'd just gone through general assignment to some other colony. I did that because I thought you could be useful here. If you're not going to be useful, you can move out to one of the section villages tomorrow. Now, I'm not asking you what you saw. I'm asking you to tell me what the things you saw might mean, as far as the ability of the Meda V'Dan to fight goes. Stop for a minute, now, and think. Then see if you can't come up with something to justify the job I've given you."

Spal hesitated.

"There's . . . nothing," he said, his voice tight. "That's the truth. There just isn't anything to tell you. Oh, that town of theirs isn't built to be any kind of a defence point, but what can I tell about what they might have hidden away there in the way of armament?"

"Just a minute," said Mark. "What's this about the Meda V'Dan city not being built as a defence point? What do you mean?"

Spal shrugged.

"Well, it's plain enough to see," he said. "Those buildings of theirs, and most of the stuff in them, aren't heavy and thick enough to stand up to more than a few seconds of heat from even the small fixed plasma rifles on our scout ships. You noticed how flimsy everything was built? And they don't have any protection from the terrain, like being down in a cup-valley or something so they'd have hills around to give them a high horizon; they're deliberately built out in the flat open, with the ground even slagged around them. Even if they've got real weapon power tucked away out of sight there, it doesn't make sense laying themselves out in the open like that, and building with such light metal they'd lose a lot of their city even if they drove off or killed an attack force."

"Hell," put in Brot, "maybe they're so sure they can knock off an enemy before he even gets close that they don't have to worry about getting damaged. Maybe they've got some kind of weapon tucked away we've never dreamed of."

"When I was in the Marines, our intelligence people didn't think so," said Spal. "And anyway, they've not only built as if they didn't worry about being hurt. It's almost as if they deliberately hunted up the most open, defenceless place to build in."

"Maybe there's something close by they need," grunted the crippled station commander.

"No," said Mark, "I was looking for signs of civilization on the planet as we went in, and I didn't see any, except for that one city. There's nothing around it, either, not even what you might expect in the way of farmland. Did you see anything else, Spal?"

"No," said Spal.

"Maybe, all this time, they've just had an outpost there," Brot muttered.

"Pretty big for just an outpost," said Spal.

"I think so, too," said Mark, thoughtfully. "That city was big enough to hold at least a million Meda V'Dan. Twenty-five square miles of ten-story buildings is a lot of buildings."

"If they live there," said Brot, "they've got

to have some way of feeding themselves."

"They're omnivores like us," said Mark. "You know when they raid, along with tools, equipment, and weapons, they usually take any stored grain or harvested agricultural products. Assuming they get part of the nutriments they want from outside, mainly the carbohydrate part, they could grow their protein indoors under laboratory conditions. In fact, with all the evidence of technology they've got kicking around, that might be the easiest method for them. We know they can eat our food in a pinch—as long as it isn't seasoned in any way—but no human I ever heard of knows what their food looks like. It could be almost completely synthetic."

"Why?" asked Brot bluntly. "Why synthesize when growing's simpler?"

"I don't know," said Mark. "But if they do, the reason for their doing it could tell us a lot about them. Particularly if we could find out why they build the kind of city they do, and tie the two reasons together."

The three of them talked a while longer, and Mark tried to stimulate Spal to additional useful deductions about what he had seen, but without results. They split up, and Mark went to see Lily in the underground records room.

He found her working alone there, recording a report on what she had seen on the Meda V'Dan visit. She smiled up at him and switched off the machine as he came in and took a chair facing her.

"You're pleased," she said.

"I think you've got a little more imagination and initiative than Spal," he answered. He told her what Spal had been able to come up with in the way of observations upon the Meda V'Dan.

"How about you?" he wound up. "What were you able to deduce about the philosophy and character of the Meda V'Dan?"

"I'm sorry," she said, and she looked sorry as she said it. "I'd like to tell you I came up with something vital and unknown about them, but I didn't. Oh, I'll get together with my assistants and we'll go over this report I'm doing and see if we don't find something useful psychologically or sociologically from what I saw and remember. But all I can really tell you about the Meda V'Dan after seeing them is that, one, they scare me silly, and, two, I don't see how you could be so sure you could bluff them the way you did."

"They bluff, too," Mark said.

"I suppose they do." She stared at him, her small face serious. "But I certainly didn't get the feeling they were bluffing. I got the feeling they believe everything they say about themselves."

"Such as?"

"Well, that business of their being an old race when our race was young," she said. "The business of being older than any other race in the universe and that they were going to go on living even after we were dead."

He looked at her sharply.

"You didn't tell me you could understand

Meda V'Dan speech," he said.

"If you'd asked me on the ship coming out here, I'd have told you," she said. "I didn't think of it then as something that might be helpful to get you to choose me. I didn't think of it at all until you put me to work to find out about the Meda V'Dan. Then I was a little afraid to tell you because, to tell the truth"— she hesitated—"I don't really understand the language all that well. It's just that I picked up a sort of working knowledge of it, along with a lot of other languages I was learning so I could read and appreciate the philosophy of the people who spoke them. And it got to be something of a hobby with me."

"I see. All right," he said. "But the point is you believed the Meda V'Dan about this business of their race living forever? Because of some secret they had, wasn't it?" She nodded. "Why? What made you believe them? That's the sort of thing any race might like to think about itself?"

"I don't know . . ." She frowned. "It's just that it seemed to fit in. I suppose it was just a subconscious reaction of mine to how it seemed to match with everything else there. The idea of their having a secret and living forever seemed to tie up, somehow, with the way they were, and the way they lived. It was only a feeling, but I had it."

He was watching her closely.

"Well, hang on to it," he said. "Think about it some more and see if something in the way of concrete evidence doesn't come to mind. One of the things I learned from Wilkes

Danielson—he was my tutor, back at the Earth-City—was that the hunches of a trained observer are likely to be a lot closer to the truth than anyone untrained would guess. An experienced observer picks up all sorts of little signals from an observed situation without being consciously aware of them as specifics, Wilkes said. And from what I've seen, he's probably right."

Mark got to his feet.

"Can't you stay awhile?" she asked.

"Too much to do," he said. "We've got a week's work to get done in a couple of days, and I need to be on top of everything that is done."

He went out.

He had not exaggerated the work needed and the time needed to do it, and as it turned out it was accomplished with only about fifteen minutes to spare.

He was sitting slumped in the chair at his desk in the unlighted Residence office two and a half days later, dawn greying the sky above black clumps of Earth-imported pines beyond the tall Residence window, when Ulla Showell came to find him. At the sound of footsteps, he looked up, numb with fatigue through all his body, but his mind clear with that abnormal, last-ditch clarity that comes shortly before the point of physical collapse. He saw her standing just beyond the desk, the white dress around her slim young body seeming to float by itself in the dim, dark room.

"They told me you'd headed for bed," she

said. "So I looked for you in your room first. When you weren't there, I guessed I'd find you stopped somewhere along the way."

"I said I was going to bed to shut them up," he answered. He pointed a finger toward a chair alongside the desk, facing him. "Sit down."

He reached wearily for the light button on the desk.

"Leave the light off," she said. "It's peaceful here in the dark."

He nodded, drew back his hand, and let it drop off the desk edge onto his knee.

"Why don't you go to bed?" she asked.

"I'm still awake," he said. "And there's still things to be done."

"There'll always be things to be done," she said.

"Yes."

He was too tired to ask her why she had come looking for him. He simply waited. But that was a mistake. As they sat there in the gloom, her physical presence only a few feet from him began to reach him even through his exhaustion. There was something about this girl, the very fact of her existence, that seemed to invite him to question everything he had committed himself to do ever since he could remember. Why? His mind, usually so unsparing facing questions, seemed to duck and dodge aside from this one. It was not just that—face it, he told himself—he was strongly attracted to her as a girl, a woman, or rather would be if he let himself be. It was something more than that. Something about her challenged him to prove that there was no mistake somewhere in his planning.

He jerked his thoughts angrily away from that subject. There was no sense in sitting here, letting himself be silently hypnotized by her presence. To force her to break that silence he spoke up himself, brusquely.

"Well?" he said. "What brings you here?"

"I told Dad I wanted to make a visit to Abruzzi Station to see Jarl," she answered. "I even said I might be thinking of marrying Jarl."

"Marry him!" Mark was jolted out of his exhaustion and introspection alike by the idea. It was like a cold hand clutching at his stomach, and his thoughts whirled.

"Why not? It could be done, couldn't it?" she said. "As acting station commander you can marry colonists, can't you?"

"I wouldn't," he said.

"You wouldn't? Why not?"

He had his spinning thoughts under control now.

"I also have to approve such marriages," he said. "I wouldn't approve this one. I need Jarl."

"What if I were willing to pay?" she said. He peered at her in the gloom, wishing he could make out the expression on her face. "Credit, old Navy ships, equipment—anything."

"We're past the point of needing anything like that," Mark said. "We're at the point now where what we need most is to make our own way as a colony with what we've already got.

For that, we need Jarl.''

"You wouldn't be losing Jarl. You'd be gain-ing me.''

"I don't want you—I mean I don't want you here as one of the colonists,'' Mark said harsh-ly. "For one thing, you'd never fit in.''

"We'll see about that,'' she said. "I've got Navy permission to visit as long as I like. See if you still feel I won't fit in in a month or two from now.''

Inexplicably, he felt as if she were driving him against a wall.

"For another thing,'' he said recklessly, "you don't want Jarl.'' The words came tumbling out angrily, surprising him. Some-how she seemed able to provoke him into speaking out about his most private beliefs. "You've talked yourself into wanting him just to soothe your conscience. Most of you Earth-City aristocrats don't even have a conscience, but you do, and you think you can settle it after seeing the colonists on the ship on the way out here, and places like this station, and Navy Base the way you must know it is, by doing something for Jarl Rakkal, as if he were some special victim of the situation. But he's not. There's no more tragedy about his being lotteried than about any other colonist. The best thing you can do is stop playing games, go back to Earth, and just forget about the Colonies. Put it all out of your mind the way all your friends back there do.''

He stopped talking. The effort behind his words had pulled him upright in his chair. The day was breaking fast, and now he could make out not only the expression on her face but the dark shadows under her eyes. Only, seeing her expression was no help. He found it unreadable.

She did not answer him for a moment. When she did, her voice was quiet, almost remote.

"You don't understand me at all," she said.

"*I* don't understand *you*—" the accusation struck him as ridiculous.

"No. And you should," she said, in the same quiet voice.

"I should? Why?"

"Because we're a lot alike," she said. "You were an orphan, with your parents killed before you could remember them. So was I— practically. My mother died when I was born and my father was always off Earth on Navy business or away from home. We both grew up by ourselves."

"And that," he said, "makes us alike?"

"Yes," she said, "because neither of us would ever give in. I never gave up trying to make the universe come out the way I thought it ought to be. And neither have you."

He stared at her in the growing pale light of dawn, feeling once more that strange power of hers that seemed to back him against a wall.

"Of course I don't want to marry Jarl," she said. "You're right about him. But my father thinks I'm visiting here to see if I do, and you can't send me away. So I'm staying because I won't give up wanting to make things come out right. Maybe what I need to find out about how to do that is right here, in what you're doing with your colonists and your outposters. So you might as well get used to having me around."

He found his voice, at that.

"Damn it!" he said. "Do you think this is some kind of game I'm running here? Do you think the Meda V'Dan are just going to be going through the motions when they hit this station any minute now?"

He took hold of the desk edge with both hands and hauled himself to his feet.

"In fact, you ought to have been out of here a long time ago, and over in the trenches behind the trees, away from the Residence, like everyone else. Come on, I'll take you over right now."

He led her out the door. She joined him in the ground car outside without a word.

"You're an idiot," he continued harshly, as he put the car in motion and swung it toward the dark, distant clump of trees. "Even if you want to set the universe right, you've got to face the fact that the universe is people. And to change people—for good or bad—costs. You'd better count that cost before you go charging out to fix things."

"As you have?" she said.

"Yes," he answered. His jaw was set so hard the muscles were aching. "People worship's not a bad religion once you get it through your head that your god-object's got all the faults any single human ever had. So don't expect people to act like gods, or even like noblemen, just because you've helped them on their way toward heaven. The human animal's what it always was, and the important thing is to save people's lives and souls if you can, not that they lie, cheat, take bribes, or kill. Because they'll turn on you when you've done your best for them and hang you high in the sun as a warning to anyone else who thinks the worship of one's fellowman is a soft and easy service! And you can count on that!''

Once more as the words leaped from him, he had time to feel surprise at the way she could trigger off the utterance of his private thoughts. Having spoken, he shrank a little inside himself, in anticipation of what she would say to this latest bit of self-confession. But the answer he flinched from never came. They were only halfway across the open ground to the trees when the warning siren whooped.

CHAPTER TWELVE

Mark wrenched the controls of the ground car, and it jerked about, almost throwing Ulla out. She clung to the handrail on the fire wall before her as the vehicle raced toward a different patch of wood some three quarters of a mile from the station buildings. They slid in among the trees, leaving a trail of dust and disturbed ground litter like smoke in the air behind them. Mark jerked the car to a stop beside an open, circular pit about five feet deep in which Paul sat surrounded by a ring of sensory equipment hastily pulled from its proper building back at the station.

Mark jumped from the car before it had actually stopped shuddering from the hard back air blast that had halted it. He dropped into the pit beside Paul.

"What've you got?" he asked.

"Three," answered Paul without looking up. "Coming up planetary in orbit around east sunside, velocity four, acceleration none, mass eighteen."

Mark glanced into the scan cube and saw the three points of light to which Paul referred. An orbit velocity of four and no comparable acceleration of the three Meda V'Dan ships would mean that they had already killed their interworld true speed and achieved orbit on the night side of Garnera VI. They were coming around to the dawn line by calculation just when that would put them over Abruzzi Fourteen Station. At mass eighteen, they would be ships about double the size of the Navy scout ships and, it went without saying, with five to eight times the offensive weaponry.

Mark reached past Paul's shoulder to unhook the command phone and call the entrenched plasma rifles taken from the two scouts still on the landing area before the station. Paul was busily juggling his controls to keep the orbiting Meda V'Dan in scan—they were still a good ninety degrees or so below horizon line of sight—and he swayed his body sideways to give Mark access to the phone.

"Guns?" Mark said into the mouthpiece of the phone.

"Guns here," answered the voice of Brot.

"Attention," said Mark. "Three bandits, expected at—"

"Fourteen minutes," said Paul. "Thirteen . . ."

"In about twelve minutes," said Mark, "count from now and dropping. Spal?"

"Sir," said the ex-Marine from a speaker box before Paul, "both plasma rifles and crews ready to fire."

"Fine," said Mark. "Don't fire until I tell you. We don't want to warn them off until you can get a good shot at them."

"Understood, sir."

"Fine. Ships?"

The voice of Race answered from one of the two hidden scout ships, "Sir."

"Orval?"

"Sir," the voice of the other outposter sounded from the second ship.

"You've heard the transmissions," said Mark. "Three bandits moving this way from orbit in now ten minutes and minus. Don't move until I call you airborne, then hold air, but below the horizon until I give you the attack word. Stay a good two miles apart and don't try to take on anything more than a wounded ship close to the ground. The bandits are double your size and any of them could chew you both up in half a minute at five hundred feet of altitude. Stay low. Follow orders. Understood?"

"Understood." The answer came back from both outposters at once.

"Hand weapons," said Mark.

"Sir," responded the harsh voice of Brot, "I've been listening. All groups of gunmen dug in and ready."

"Thank you, sir," said Mark. "Wait for orders."

"Understood."

"Stand by, all," said Mark. He took the phone from his mouth and looked once more at the instruments in front of Paul. Glancing up from this, he saw Ulla still sitting frozen in the ground car.

"Get down here," he called to her. "Down inside, and sit with your back to the side of the pit, out from underfoot."

He saw that she moved to obey, and he went back to studying the instruments.

"What's the readout?" he asked Paul. Paul glanced at a silvery tape with black numbers on it, slowly spewing out of a slot in a box near his feet.

"Can't tell much," Paul answered, after a second. "Large fixed weapons both fore and aft on each ship, of course. No index on smaller weapons yet—too much distance. They'll have to drop down from orbit before we can be sure of smaller guns."

He fell silent. The minutes ticked off.

"Here comes the first one now," he said. "Others at interval—"

His words were drowned out by a thunderclap of sound. Instinctively, all three of them at the command post jerked their heads back to look upward. High against the clear, cloudless, brightening blue of the dawn sky was a black speck, almost directly overhead.

"About four thousand only. Just inside long range," the voice of Spal, finishing a sentence, was coming from the black box. "Request fire permission."

"Negative," said Mark.

There was a second thunderclap. Then a third. Three specks swam in the blue depths overhead.

"Hand-weapon groups ready," said Mark into the phone.

"Ready, sir," said Brot's voice.

One of the specks seemed to jerk away from the other two. Then it commenced falling in a long shallow curve that at first looked as if it would take the ship out of sight over the horizon. But then the speck slowed its fall and began to grow larger. It swelled before them to a dot, to an egg shape, to an oval—

"Hand-weapons group, fire at command," said Mark.

"Understood."

The tiny shape of the Meda V'Dan ship seemed just above the horizon. Suddenly, it leaped at them from that position.

"Fire!" The voice of Brot came from the loudspeaker box.

White fingers of light—bright even in the growing daylight—stretched up from the clumps of trees immediately surrounding the station, rising from all sides until they met in an apex area just above the station buildings. The light fingers hung there like a tent of searchlight beams, and the attacking Meda V'Dan ship flicked through them.

The ground jarred to the impact of another air concussion and the rolling battering of several heavy explosions. Then the attacking ship was gone and three of the station buildings, including a corner of the Residence, were burning. The flames flickered with difficulty against the smothering effect of the athermal coating, sprayed on all exposed surfaces the day before. A little smoke rose.

Down in the landing area, one of the standing scout ships showed a black gash in its side from which little flames licked.

"Cease fire," said Brot. "Report, group captains."

There was a momentary pause.

"Hand-weapons report," came Brot's voice again. "Sir, no group hit, no one hurt. Of course they didn't expect we'd be out here, firing back. Next time we'll feel it."

"Change position of groups."

"Accomplished already, sir."

"Fine. Guns?"

"Sir," said Spal's voice again.

"Stand ready," said Mark. "The bandits know we've got men with hand weapons around the station now. They'll probably try a run on all three ships first. If they do, hold your fire and leave it to hand weapons. We want to force them to come in and hang so close you can't miss, before we let them know you're there. On straight runs like these last, they'll have trouble hitting the hand-weapons positions."

"Coming," Paul's voice was almost an interruption, it followed so closely on Mark's last words to the ex-Marine. "All three!"

"Hand weapons, fire at group command," said Mark. "Guns, ships—hold fire."

The three specks were now falling toward the horizon together. There was a moment of breathless waiting, and then all three sprang past above the station at eye-baffling speed. The triple thunder of their passing concussion stunned the people on the ground.

Once more the tent of hand-weapons beams had lifted over the station buildings, and the buildings this time showed no new damage. But treetops in every clump of trees for half a mile from the station were burning.

"Cease fire," said Brot's voice. "Report, captains."

Paul grunted with satisfaction among his instruments.

"Got their index that time," he said. "Complete readout. They run four to six light weapons apiece amidships. Seventeen mounted weapons among them all."

"Ships, guns, hand weapons?" said Mark. "Did you hear that, all of you? Ships, you look out for those midship weapons in particular when you tangle with the bandits. In close, they can do as much damage as the big guns fore and aft."

"Two groups wiped out," said Brot, his hard voice unchanged in tone. "Six of ten in another. All other eight groups untouched. We hit anything?"

"Paul?" Mark looked over at the other outposter. Paul glanced over the instruments to his right.

"Readout index shows some damage to the third bandit to pass," he answered. "Hull may be pierced just ahead of the drive units. Could be crippling hit, could not. Other bandits just scarred."

"Sir," said Brot. "With permission, will change my fire patterns."

"Go ahead," said Mark.

"Thank you, sir."

"Here they come," said Paul.

Once more there was the thunder of passage

and the tent of white beams—a tent now
elongated in shape. Staring up toward the
western sky, Mark saw the three specks
climbing—the last one lagging behind the
other two.

"Think we hurt him?" Mark looked at Paul,
who frowned over his instruments.

"Index inconclusive," Paul answered.
"Could be."

"Guns," said Mark into the phone. "Alert on
next pass. We may have a cripple."

But the concussions of the next pass shook
them unchanged. And the specks climbing the
western wall of the sky afterward held tight
formation.

"Two additional groups hit hard," said
Brot. "Four lightly. Two untouched. Six
groups now operational. Moving all groups."

"Sir," said Spal. "The bandits are running
the same pattern over us each time. I can get
two of three."

"Negative," said Mark. "Repeat negative.
Your two weapons represent our only really
effective firepower source. Hold until ordered."

"Sir."

"Paul," said Mark, looking at the other outposter. "Nothing more on index about that
third bandit's damages?"

Paul shook his head.

"Coming again," he said.

"Stand by," Mark told the phone. "Hand
weapons, fire at group command. All others
hold."

Once more came the passage of the Meda

V'Dan ships. The tree clumps had also been sprayed with athermal against the Meda V'Dan fire weapons, but most of them were now blackened and scorched badly, and three of them had ceased to exist, looking as if the place of their growth had been trampled by some great, burning foot.

"Five groups operational," said Brot's unemotional voice.

"They won't keep this up too long," said Mark, half to himself, half to Paul. "They can't land as long as the hand-weapon groups are there, and they can't wipe out the hand-weapon groups without slowing down on their passes or hovering above the station." He picked up the phone.

"Guns, ships, hand weapons?" he said. "Attention, all. Be alert for a change of tactics by bandits on next pass."

"Coming," said Paul.

"On their way now," said Mark into the phone.

Triple thunder echoed as the Meda V'Dan ships flashed past at the same speed as before.

"Light hits," said Brot's voice. "All five groups still operational—*look out, they're back!*"

The Meda V'Dan ships were suddenly above the station once more. They had flipped just below the horizon level and returned. They skidded to a stop in midair, some five hundred feet above the station and its surrounding area.

"Guns!" shouted Mark. "Guns! Fire at will!"

With sizzling roars, two thick white ropes of incandescence reached up from tree clumps nearly a mile on either side of the station buildings. One Meda V'Dan ship, touched squarely in the belly by the discharge of the fixed weapon on the command post side of the station, fell out of formation immediately, yawing and corkscrewing earthward until it landed in a long slewed slide and lay still, a black smoking gape in its hull.

The ship touched by the far plasma rifle slewed about and lost altitude, but then pulled up and tried to turn back away from the position of the rifle that had damaged it. But this brought it again over the station, and the hand weapons scored it.

"Ships!" Mark was shouting into the phone. "A cripple! Take it! Quick—but keep low."

He glanced at the third, the untouched Meda V'Dan vessel which was now climbing swiftly, unhurt, into the eastern sky. But it showed no sign of turning back to rescue its partner ships.

"Paul, monitor that one getting away," said Mark. His voice was drowned in the howl of torn air as the two hidden scout ships flashed into view over the horizon.

At the sight of them, the cripple tried once more, desperately, to gain altitude. But the effort evidently exhausted its damaged drive capabilities. Its nose dropped and it went earthward in a long slant to avoid the guns of the two scout ships closing in upon it.

"Cease fire, ships! Cease fire, all but hand weapons covering downed bandits!" shouted Mark into the phone. "Hand weapons covering ships hold fire but return any fire from bandits."

He turned to Paul.

"What about the third one?"

"Going . . . gone," said Paul, pointing at the scan tube. "He's not even stopping to orbit out."

Mark straightened up. For the first time he realized he had spent the whole time of the battle crouched over the phone and the instruments. His back felt stiff and painful, and when he closed his mouth after speaking, his teeth gritted together.

He became conscious of the fact that there was dust in his mouth. In fact, the whole area between himself and the station—and probably beyond as well for an equal distance—was hazed with smoke and dust. He looked at Paul and saw what the other man was grey-faced with dust, as was Ulla, when he turned to look at her.

She was sitting motionless against the vertical dirt wall of the pit, as if she, as well as he, had held the same position all through the battle. He stepped over to her and held out his hand.

"It's all over," he said. "I'll take you back to the Residence now—or someplace else if that's been burned out."

She took his hand and let him lift her to her feet without a word.

"Be with you in a second," he said. "You can get in the ground car."

He turned back to Paul, who was pulling connections on some of the communications equipment that was now out of operation.

"Better keep somebody on watch at the scan cube for the next few days, just in case," Mark said. "The rest of the equipment can go back up to the station without waiting."

Paul nodded.

Mark turned away and went back to Ulla, who was brushing dust from her hands and face. Silently, they climbed out of the pit and got into the ground car together. Mark put the vehicle in motion, swung it around, and headed back toward the Residence.

Ulla said nothing until they were almost back at the Residence, which it seemed had suffered only the mild initial damage sustained on the first Meda V'Dan pass. But when she did speak, her words were disconcerting.

"That business you mentioned about people hanging you high in the sun when they were through with you, to teach others that they weren't easy to serve," she said. "Do you really expect something like that to happen to you some day?"

He looked at her, but her face was honestly troubled and questioning.

"I don't just think it might," he said. "I know it will."

She looked to the front again, and a moment later he drew the car up in front of the main door of the Residence. She got out without either of them saying any more to each other, and he wheeled the car away to supervise the beginning of the cleanup—for a little while before exhaustion finally claimed its right and sent him staggering to his bed.

CHAPTER THIRTEEN

"There's a way around it," said Mark.

He sat drinking crushed rum cocktails with Admiral-General Jaseth Showell in the wide, softly carpeted living room of Showell's suite at Navy Base HQ. Ulla was across the room. A ten-by-twelve-foot sealed window gave a view of the square miles of airless space occupied by the ranked spaceships, docks, barracks, administrative and hospital structures that made up Outer Navy Base. The light of the GA star, which Navy slang had nicknamed "Murgatroyd's Onion," shone unchangeably upon this multitude of metal bodies, the larger ones with checkerboard hulls of alternate silver and black squares.

"You and I know," Mark went on, "that they're liable to distort things back at the Earth-City because they don't understand what it's like out here."

"Yes," murmured Jaseth. The little grey-headed man was watching Mark with the polite but unwinking interest of a robin examining a working mound of soft ground that night at any moment reveal a worm.

"Nobody could be more pleased than we are —my foster father and I," said Mark, "by the flattering attention we've been getting back at the Earth-City since we captured those Meda V'Dan renegades. I ought to include the way the other outposters at the station feel about that. I might even throw in our colonists, too. They've really had a shot in the arm. Production's way up. And of course that's what we're all out here for—to get production up and our Colonies standing on their own feet."

"Of course," said Jaseth, nodding.

"But, nice as it is," said Mark, "I mean the praise from Earth, the attention, even the reparations the Meda V'Dan were so generous as to pay when we handed back the renegades and their two ships—there's a drawback to it all. It puts Abruzzi Fourteen a little too much in the spotlight. We're working hard to improve things so this colony of ours can stand on its own feet, but production or crop failures, or any of a dozen things, can always trip us up. And if something like that does, there are people back on Earth in government who may blame it on the fact this business of driving off the renegade Meda V'Dan has gone to our heads."

"Always possible, yes," said Jaseth.

"But there could be an answer to it that'd also be an answer to these people back at the Earth-City who don't seem to understand how we happened to have four small Navy ships without Navy men to man them," Mark said.

"In fact, it's the sort of answer that could solve all our problems, past and future."

"And future?" said Jaseth.

"You know," said Mark, shrugging, "it's simply a matter of your telling Navy HQ back on Earth that your letting us have the four ships was part of a quiet experiment on your part in furthering the self-sufficiency of the Colonies like ours. After all, that's essentially what it was. You might even ask permission to extend the experiment by making more ships available to us and other Colonies. Not only would it look good, but it would reduce the pressure on your own duty ships to protect against the Meda V'Dan renegades."

"More ships and weapons?" Jaseth shook his head slowly. "No, I don't think so. But your other suggestion isn't bad. I think—"

"It'd be useless without some concrete new evidence to back it up," Mark said. "After all, Abruzzi Fourteen probably invited retaliation from other renegade Meda V'Dan because of the way we treated those three ships. It wouldn't do to have us hit again, and this time be wiped out for lack of the necessary defensive equipment. Also, it'd look unnatural if, your experiment having worked, you didn't continue to push it forward vigorously. Above all, we just might find ourselves being visited by some news people from Earth, and the sight of recently arrived equipment and military supplies would go a long way toward filling in any gaps there might be in the memories of my people about your intention to help from the very start."

"Of course," said Jaseth, frowning at his cocktail glass. "Earth HQ might not approve . . ."

"They can hardly avoid approving, can they?" Mark said. "With all this publicity, which goes a long way in answering some of the Navy's government critics who've been complaining about inactivity at the Base here?"

"But, then," said Jaseth, glancing over at Ulla, who with her own cocktail glass was sitting silently apart, listening, "there's that matter of your going to a home world of the Meda V'Dan the way you did, almost inviting a raid."

"I don't find anything in the law or Colony Regulations against it," said Mark. "And of course we've been assured by your Navy people for years that the Meda V'Dan are completely peaceful and friendly—with the exception, of course, of occasional renegades."

"Nonetheless," said Jaseth. "You were undoubtedly aware that you were taking a risk."

"Oh, certainly," said Mark. "We might have run into renegades on the way there, for example. Luckily, however, we made it safely and even set up a profitable trade pact with the peaceful authorities of the Meda V'Dan— a pact we'll have to carry through now, naturally, if we don't want to offend them. But you're right about all this attracting more attention from renegades. Come to think of it, that makes it all the more important that the colony gets more ships, and larger ones, as soon as possible. I'm indebted to you for pointing it out."

"I don't believe I did. It was your conclusion," said Jaseth mildly. He put his glass
down on the low table between their chairs.
"Still, I'll have to think this matter over. How
about it? Shall we go to dinner now?"

The three of them got up and went into the
adjoining dining room, talking about other
things. Ulla took part easily in this conver-
sation. She had come here with Mark five
days before, and already intimated that she
would be going back with him to Abruzzi
Station. Since that first morning before the
raid, they had talked privately again. Mark
did not know whether what he had said to her
had gotten through or not. But she had been
undeniably helpful to him here at the Base in
his dealings with her father and other Navy
officers. Only, he caught her watching him at
odd times, as if she were secretly observing
him.

He had not said anything more to her about
anything important. There had been no
apparent need, and besides, he had been left
with the feeling that he had said too much already. Frankly, he admitted to being afraid
that if he started to talk to her on any matters,
his tongue might run away with him again,
and this time there was no telling what he
might find himself saying. He reminded himself harshly that his future was short in any
case, and held no room for women, and so
tried to put Ulla completely from his mind.

The other dinner guests—some twenty Base
officers, a few wives, and a couple of impor-

tant salesmen—stood and applauded briefly, Navy fashion, as their host, his daughter, and the other guest of honour entered. Jaseth took the head of the long, narrow table, seating Mark on his right and Ulla on his left. On the other side of Mark was a general of the Marines whom Mark had met two days before at the cocktail party that had celebrated Mark's arrival.

"Hear you're leaving at the end of the week," the Marine general said to Mark, once they were all seated.

"That's right," Mark nodded.

"Too bad." The general was a tall man in his late twenties, already running to fat. "If you could just wait around until the first of next week, we could start hosting you all over again when Taraki—admiral-general of the Red—starts his tour at the Base and Jaseth, here, goes home." The general looked across at Jaseth. "How about it, Jaseth? Talk Mark into staying into next week, will you?"

"Doubt if I could," Jaseth said.

"No," grumbled the Marine general, cheerfully, "because you don't care enough. You're headed home. How about the rest of us who have to stay here?"

"Don't let it prey on you, Johnny," said Jaseth. "You've got only four months to go before you'll be headed home, too."

"Four months! Two thirds of a tour of duty! Damn you, Jaseth, you talk like it was three days!"

Jaseth laughed and turned to Ulla.

"He doesn't care," said Johnny, leaning

confidentially close to Mark, and nodding at Jaseth. "I won't either, when I get to be admiral-general. Meanwhile, it's nothing but duty, duty, duty—double duty, thanks to you and your Meda V'Dan, damn it."

"Thanks to me?" Mark asked. Johnny had been making the acquaintance of more than one crushed rum during the before-dinner hour, and his breath was heavy at this conspiratorial distance.

"Thanks to the fuss back at Earth-City you kicked up by nailing a couple of renegade ships," he said, "now we've got patrol exercises. Patrol exercises, damn it! Can you imagine a bunch, any bunch, of EmVeeDee renegades with the guts to hit a Navy wing on *patrol?* They learned better than that forty years ago. Besides—shouldn't tell you this. Restricted information, but hell, you're on our side—we've already sent confidential word to the EmVeeDee authorities telling them there's a real stink being kicked up by that raid on you, and for once they've got to sit on their renegades for a while."

"What do you think?" said Mark. "Do you think the Meda V'Dan authorities will do it?"

"Why, hell, yes!" muttered Johnny. He lowered his voice still further. "You know as well as I do, that's a lot of whatever-you-want-to-call-it, their not being able to hold down their renegades when they want to. We know that. They know we know it. And usually we get along just fine. Hell, nobody minds a few stations being hit from time to time—say a couple a month. That's all in the statistics.

No offence, I know you're an outposter yourself. But you've had a good Earth-City education. You know we can't go to war over a
few casualties a week. You understand that."

"I've seen it," said Mark.

"There. Said you'd understand. What I say
myself, let the damn aliens nibble a bit from
time to time and they won't get hungry
enough to take a big bite. But at the same
time, hell, if they make a mistake and a lot of
fuss is made about one of their raids, then
they've got to play ball with us until things
calm down again. That's just common sense.
Right?"

"Right," said Mark.

"And those EmVeeDee's have got it—common sense I mean," said Johnny, "when it
comes to looking after their own interest.
They may be aliens, but they've got common
sense. Do you want to hand down the wine
bottle there? Seems like I'm empty here
again."

Mark passed the bottle.

He spent another five days mainly in attend-
ing day and evening social occasions at the
base. He said no more to Jaseth, however,
about the added ships for which he had asked.
But on the evening of the sixth day—just before the morning on which Jaseth was to return to Earth until his next tour of duty as the
Base commanding officer, six months hence—
he drew Mark aside during a small party in
the Officers Club.

"I'd thought Ulla might want to go back to
Earth with me when I go," the older man said.

"But it seems she wants to stay out here at your station. That worries me a little. After all, you've already been raided once."

"I don't think we'll be raided again," said Mark.

"But," said Jaseth, "you've asked me for these ships—"

"I asked for the ships with the general situation in mind," said Mark, meeting the older man's eyes. "Ulla's staying is a specific matter."

"Ah . . . she tells me Jarl Rakkal . . ." Jaseth hesitated. For a moment the older man seemed genuinely sincere and concerned. "I don't suppose you could tell me—"

"I have my hands full with the station and the colony," said Mark coldly.

"Oh? I see. Well"—Jaseth's voice was relieved—"you'll be glad to hear I've finally decided to let you have the ships and materials you asked for—"

"And cadre personnel to train my colonists in handling them?" said Mark.

"Cadre?" Jaseth looked sharply at him. "Oh, no, not that. I can explain ships back on Earth. I can explain that this was a secret project of mine and that's why you didn't admit to it sooner. I can justify more ships and any amount of supplies you want. But Navy personnel—no. HQ's not going to have any objection to your colonists making themselves useful, but it's the Navy keeps the peace here in outer space. The Navy, and no one else!"

"The ships'll have to do, then," said Mark.

"I want regulation cruiser class vessels, mass forty—twelve of them."

"Twelve? A wing and a half?" Jaseth stared. "You can't crew that many. Not if half your colonists were rated spacemen!"

"I'll take them anyway," said Mark. They looked at each other. "If I did that without asking you, it'd be six months before you even noticed they were gone from this base."

Slowly, Jaseth nodded.

"I'll make out the orders tonight," he said. "You can start moving them out tomorrow— with your own crews and officers."

"That's why I brought along three scout ships when I came," Mark said. "I've got my navigator and enough people to lift the extra ships and set them down on Garnera Six— and that's all it takes."

Two days later, however, when the twelve heavy vessels and the three scouts were back in space and well away from observation on the scan cubes of Navy Base, Mark called Maura Vols into the command area from the spacious room she now occupied as navigator and position officer in the cruiser Mark had chosen to use as flagship.

"We'll change our destination point now," he told her. "From Garnera Six to Point One, in that list of destination codes I gave you."

Ulla, who was with him in the command area, looked about sharply at his words.

"The whole wing to Point One?" Maura asked. She had become crisp and self-assured, and she no longer recalculated several times before ordering a position shift.

"The wing and the scouts—all of us," said Mark. Ulla came over as Maura turned and went out of the room.

"Point One?" Ulla asked. "What's that? Or shouldn't I ask?"

"When I went to see the Meda V'Dan," Mark said, "I agreed to a trading deal with them involving sixty-seven pieces of handicraft made by my colonists. Point One is the space point where we were to meet them to exchange goods."

She looked startled.

"You think they'll be there—after what you did to those three alien ships that tried to raid Abruzzi Station?"

"Absolutely," said Mark. "One of the main principles of the Meda V'Dan is that there's no connection or responsibility between separate acts by different individuals. The ones we'll meet are going to act as if they never heard of the three ships that tried to raid Abruzzi Fourteen, and all we have to do is do the same."

"Even when you show up with twelve full cruisers?"

"We won't show up with twelve all at once," said Mark. "We'll move in just one ship to begin with and then add others."

When they came to the edge of the cruiser's scan-cube range, Mark paused to locate the Meda V'Dan. They were discovered after a six-hour search—three mass-thirty-six ships, only slightly smaller than Mark's cruisers, waiting for contact. Three such ships were several times the strength needed to handle four heavy scouts such as Abruzzi Station had proved to have during the raid, and the addition of a single mass-forty cruiser to reinforce the scouts still left the Meda V'Dan ships with a comfortable edge in weapons and armour for any spatial confrontation.

Therefore, the three alien ships showed no alarm when Mark's cruiser appeared alone on a short shift to within laser talk-beam range.

"Meda V'Dan," said Mark, when the beam was stabilized, "this is Outposter Station Commander Mark Ten Roos with the pieces of art we agreed to trade you. Do you have the flame handguns you agreed to trade us in exchange?"

There was a moment's pause, filled by the hiss and crackle of minor interference, for the talk beam was close to its extreme range. Then a heavy-voiced Meda V'Dan answered.

[I am the Lord and Great Captain Fateful Dreaming Man,] the Meda V'Dan said. [I and my two brother Lords and Great Captains bring you the finest of hand weapons for that which you bring us in exchange. But if your trade items are in any way deficient, take warning. You will be charged proportionately for whatever value you have attempted to cheat us by.]

"I can't object to that," said Mark. "So, I'll just give you the same warning, and charge you the same way, if your weapons strike me as being deficient in value."

[Do not be presumptuous,] retorted the voice of Fateful Dreaming Man. [It is for us to judge the bargain and you to be judged—]

The Meda V'Dan's voice broke off abruptly. Two more of Mark's cruisers had shifted into positions flanking the row of Meda V'Dan's ships.

"Forgive me if what I said sounded like presumption," said Mark. "I only meant to suggest that everything ought to be equal. Certainly you agree to that?"

Three more ex-Navy cruisers appeared together behind the Meda V'Dan ships.

There was silence from the speaker jacked into the talk-beam receiver aboard Mark's cruiser. It lasted for the tense space of perhaps two minutes while the skeleton crews aboard the human vessels counted the seconds one by one.

[I will accept your explanation,] rattled the speaker suddenly. [You may board the centre of our three vessels with three individuals bearing your trade items.]

"No," said Mark. "You can board my first vessel to appear here with one individual, after you've floated the containers of your hand weapons across to us and we've inspected them. And unless the Lord and Great Captain Fateful Dreaming Man doesn't care to risk himself personally, I suggest he be the individual."

[The Lord and Great Captain Fateful Dreaming Man,] retorted the speaker immediately, [is beyond and above and unknowing of risk. But he receives guests in courtesy and visits only in courtesy. Let him be received in courtesy, and Fateful Dreaming Man will enter your ship either alone or in company.]

"We're courteous," said Mark. "We're always courteous to our good friends the Meda V'Dan."

[I will come.]

Fateful Dreaming Man was as good as his promise, once Mark had examined the flame weapons and found them all new and in good order. The Meda V'Dan captain rode across from his ship to Mark's cruiser in a one-man safety boat, and accepted the box containing the small carved elephants from Mark's hands. He opened the box and examined them, carefully and individually, then put them all back into the box. An agreement was made for another trade in four weeks.

[We are agreed,] he said. [I will go back to my ship.]

"Just one thing," said Mark. The alien waited. "I want you to carry a message for me back to the Meda V'Dan. The ships of our Navy are going to be in space more in the near future than they have been for some years. Tell your people not to worry about any renegade Meda V'Dan who might make the mistake of attacking these Navy ships. Such renegades will have me to deal with—and I'll follow them anywhere I have to, to take care of them. Will you remember to tell your people that?"

Fateful Dreaming Man glanced across the cruiser control area to the scan cube in which the lights of his three ships burned, surrounded by the lights of Mark's six larger vessels.

[I will remember,] the Meda V'Dan said,

[and tell them.]

"Good," said Mark. "So will I. And just to make sure, I'll be reminding your people each time they come to trade with me."

The Meda V'Dan left. Mark turned to Maura Vols.

"Home," he ordered.

CHAPTER FOURTEEN

When they landed back at Abruzzi Station
with four of the big cruisers—the other eight
having been dispersed in wooded areas of the
station where they would be hidden—there
was a fine-boned, dark skinned man, slightly
taller but much more frail-looking than
Jaseth Showell, among those waiting to welcome them. This man sought out Mark among
those leaving the flagship vessel.

"Mark!" he said, reaching out both hands to
take Mark's arms like someone whose eye-
sight is no longer reliable.

"Wilkes," said Mark, and found himself
smiling at the older man. He turned to Ulla.

"Ulla, this is my Earthside tutor, Wilkes
Danielson," he said. "Wilkes, this is Ulla
Showell."

"How do you do, Miss Showell, how do you
do?" said Wilkes, letting go of Mark to shake
hands warmly with Ulla. He turned back to
Mark. "Forgive me—"

"For showing up here?" said Mark.. "I've

been expecting you.''

"Expecting me?" said Wilkes, in a tone of delight. He fell into step with Mark and Ulla as they moved to a waiting ground car and climbed in, with Mark behind the controls. Ulla took a seat in the back and motioned Wilkes to sit beside Mark, which he did.

"You used to climb mountains," Mark said. "Remember telling me about that?"

"Yes. Yes, of course—you're right," said Wilkes. "But I'm an old man now, or I thought I was an old man until I guessed what you were up to out here."

Mark swung the car about and headed toward the Residence.

"What am I up to?" he asked.

"You're making a revolution, of course!" said Wilkes. "I should have guessed it even before I read about your station driving off a Meda V'Dan ship and capturing two others. No other Outpost Station or colony has ever done anything like that, and yours couldn't have done it unless it had weapons no Outpost Station has ever had."

"It's time for a change," said Mark.

"Of course," said Wilkes. "And I should have seen it before you. I was the anthropologist, the sociologist. But then you're the one who's making it change, Mark, and that's the difference."

"So you came out to watch?" asked Mark, pulling the car to a halt before the Residence entrance.

"I came out to help. I had to pull all kinds of strings. But if a year or two is all the time I've got left, at least I can do something with it, this way. You can use me, can't you, Mark?"

"Always," said Mark. "You and Brot are part of everything I do."

He got out of the car and waited while Wilkes and Ulla also got out. They started into the Residence.

"I've got to go and talk to Brot first," Mark said, as they went through the door. "You don't mind waiting fifteen or twenty minutes, do you, Wilkes? Then I'll be free."

"Don't worry," said Ulla unexpectedly. "I'll entertain Mr. Danielson. There's a lot I want to ask him." She took the fragile older man by an arm. "We can have some coffee in the downstairs lounge here."

She led Wilkes off through a doorway to their right. Mark continued on to the entrance to Brot's room and found his adoptive father sitting up behind a desk in a power chair.

"How'd it go?" Brot asked as Mark entered the room.

"Twelve ships," said Mark. "All cruiser mass forty. And the trade went off as scheduled with the Meda V'Dan. How's it been back here?"

"Busy," growled Brot. "I'll say one thing for that Jarl—he doesn't sit around. And now that tutor of yours showing up here in the middle of everything."

"Wilkes is a walking library," said Mark quietly, sitting down in a chair opposite the desk. "And he's got true genius-level intelligence. Did he rub you the wrong way?"

"No," said Brot. "He's all right. But he's

nothing but a goddam bag of bones."

"He's dying," said Mark. "Bone cancer."

"I knew that eight years ago when I messaged him asking him to take you on for tutoring," said Brot. "But he looks like he won't last the week, now. A sneeze would tear him apart."

"He'll last long enough," said Mark. He looked at Brot. "How about you?"

"*Me?*" Brot snorted. "I'll make a hundred and thirty or blow my own brains out! You aren't classing me with someone like that?"

Mark smiled for the second time in one day —in fact, he realized, the second time since getting off the cruiser.

"I've never classed you with anyone," Mark said. "You're all by yourself, Brot."

"Too damn right. What's next in the plans?"

"Work." Mark's smile vanished. "We've got perhaps three months to train colonists to handle all twelve of those ships, at least under certain specific, simple conditions. At the end of that time, I want to hold a meeting here of all Outpost Station commanders you think would be able to work with us without fighting—either us or each other."

"I'll make a list," said Brot. "What else?"

"Minor things," said Mark. They talked a while longer about those minor things before Mark excused himself to get back to his reunion with Wilkes.

In the weeks that followed, Mark's former tutor fitted effectively and powerfully into the team Mark had set up with Lily Betaugh to deduce the philosophy and psychology of the

Meda V'Dan. Wilkes was also unexpectedly useful in that he swept up Ulla to work as his assistant. This settled an inner question Mark had been avoiding with some difficulty—which was what the daughter of Admiral General Showell was doing making an apparently unlimited stay at Abruzzi Fourteen Station. Ulla had been useful before this as a companion to Brot. But except for the lack of the parts of his limbs that had been amputated, the burly former station commander (for Mark had been confirmed in that post following the publicity about the Meda V'Dan raid) was now so stubbornly recovered that it was ridiculous to pretend he needed someone hovering about him.

But Ulla, it turned out after Wilkes had put her actively to work, had other uses as well. She was able to give Mark a rough but effective idea of where the Navy patrols would be conducting their sweeps in the neighbourhood of the Colony Worlds they were supposed to protect. From this, and working with Maura Vols, Mark was able to make an intelligent guess at which patrol the Meda V'Dan might hit if they chose to attack any part of the Navy.

"But what I can't see," protested Ulla, some nine weeks later, "is why you think they're liable to attack Navy ships at all. They never have, not since the early days of the Colonies when the Navy was first set up, and even the Navy used to say those attacks were more than likely mistakes. Once the Base was fully operational, no Meda V'Dan ship has ever looked twice at a Navy vessel.''

"They may now,'' said Mark.

"But why?'' Ulla insisted. "I know that every time the station trades with Meda V'Dan you warn the aliens to leave the Navy alone. But why would they want to do anything?''

"To find out how much strength we have here at Abruzzi Fourteen,'' said Mark, at last.

She shook her head.

"Then that means every time you warn them, you're essentially daring them to do something to a Navy patrol,'' she said. "Isn't that right?''

"Yes,'' said Mark. He discovered his jaw was set so hard that the muscles ached.

"But the colonists you're training aren't anywhere near ready to fight their ships, let alone in a space battle.''

"Give them another month,'' said Mark, "and they'll be good enough—for my purposes.''

He turned and left her. He found himself torn, these days, between the desire to seek her out and the desire to avoid her. The end result was that he buried himself in work as much as possible, and with one exception, no one at Abruzzi Fourteen came close to matching the hours he put in.

That exception was Jarl Rakkal. There was a relentlessness in the way the big man attacked any problem, but it was a smooth, efficient relentlessness that never seemed to exhaust its possessor. Four hours sleep a night were evidently sufficient for him, and during the other sixteen hours of the twenty-hour day on Garnera VI he did not let up for a second.

He made plans, then went to the place where the plans were being executed and stood over whoever was concerned with executing them until they were done to his satisfaction. He had not exaggerated to Mark his ability to handle people. He had shaken up both the agricultural and manufacturing teams of the colony and gotten them to producing at three times their former rate. He had even put Age Hammerschold in charge of the furniture factory and talked at the old man until Age stopped muttering to himself, perked up, and took command of work there.

Jarl was technically a colonist, but by sheer capability and effort he had raised himself in importance to the community, until now, with the exception of Hubble, he was the most important man after Mark at Abruzzi Fourteen. He was like a river in flood, moving everything he encountered, so that by the end of four months after he had arrived, everyone —again except for a single person—gave way to him without argument.

The exception was Brot. Against the rock that was the former station commander, the powerful waters of Jarl's will broke and divided.

"You're a smooth bastard," Brot had told him bluntly the first day they had met. "And I don't like smooth bastards. Stay out of my way and there'll be no trouble."

Jarl had refused to give up in the case of

everyone else who had resisted him. But after that first encounter with Brot he had never tried again to influence or compete with the older man. Instead he had, as Brot advised, stayed out of Brot's way. And there had been no trouble.

In a way, it was a compliment to Brot's innate strength that Jarl paid to no one else—not even to Mark. The big man was a strange case from Mark's point of view. Mark told himself that if Jarl possessed even the slightest spark of real feeling, it would have been impossible not to like him. But there was no spark. There was nothing. Jarl's concern began and ended with himself. He was without fear, brilliant, imaginative, resourceful—but within him that which should have been warm and responsive with instinctive emotions was cold and dead as some stony fossil.

Jarl recognized this in himself, obviously, because he was not shy of making comparisons between Mark and himself.

"You know," he said one day, when they had finished going over the colony's books together, "I ought to be the one to change history, not you."

Mark looked at him across the coffee pot they were sharing.

"Want to try?" Mark asked.

Jarl laughed.

"Not with hands or guns, or anything like that," he said. "But in other ways, I'm so much the better man than you—and still, there you are, out in point position for the forward march of mankind, and here I am in line behind you. And I don't have any weaknesses."

Mark drank his coffee without comment.

"What about Ulla?" asked Jarl unexpectedly.

"What about her?" Mark asked. "You don't want her."

Jarl's eyebrows went up.

"Not want Ulla? The admiral-general's daughter?" he said. "Of course I do."

"No." Mark shook his head and put his cup down. "When you first came here she might have been some help to you. You don't need her now—you're already on your way back up. So you don't want her, really."

Jarl's eyebrows came down.

"You might be right," he said. "I've got my teeth into something here. Which doesn't alter the fact that Ulla's changed now. She wants you."

Mark's jaw tightened grimly.

"I don't know that she does," he said. "But in any case, no one's going to have me."

"Still planning on dying?" Jarl considered him with a frankness as brutal as his insight was penetrating. "Excuse me. I mean still planning on being killed? What if people don't oblige you?"

Mark shoved the coffee pot and the cups to one side.

"Let's see those performance records for the spaceship trainees," he said.

"Come to think of it," said Jarl, without moving immediately, "maybe that's what it is, why you're out there in front and I'm not.

You're going someplace—to your own execution. That's why I can't beat you out. You're a moving target. If you ever stood still, I'd pass you up automatically."

"Performance records," said Mark, pointing toward the spool file drawers.

"Coming up," said Jarl, turning to get them. He got out the proper spool and snapped it into the desktop viewer, and together they bent to a study of how the training colonists to man the Navy ships was progressing.

But even though the records finally showed the trainees competent to execute the few simple ship manoeuvres that Mark required of them, that fact was not able to wash Jarl's words out of his brain. They clung there, as Jarl's words had a tendency to do, like the barbed spines of a sand burr in the skin, and they rankled. Until Mark decided that it was time to make Ulla understand about him.

He came to this conclusion while returning to the Residence unexpectedly early one day, hot and dusty from a swing by ground car around all the agricultural sections of the station. The crops were excellent this year, again thanks to Jarl. They would have more than enough to feed the colony during the winter, whose beginning was now less than three months off. But just because the harvest was good, it posed a problem. Normally, everyone in the colony who was able to work was recruited to get the crops in. But this year he had nearly a fourth of his available work force tied up in those being trained to operate, navigate, and fight the ex-Navy spaceships. If

he took them off that training and sent them
out to the fields scattered all over the station,
there could be no way of getting the ships
manned again swiftly in case of necessity.

And there had still been no sign of Meda
V'Dan activity against the Navy. The trading
ships of the aliens came right to the station
nowadays, in ever-increasing numbers, to
trade. The Meda V'Dan had never seemed so
peaceful and cooperative. And every twenty
hours one of the heavy scout ships relieved
another, out on the station by the patrol route
Mark, Maura and Ulla had decided was the
most likely area for an alien attack on the
Navy. Daily the returning scout ships report-
ed no sign of alien activity.

Mark therefore had been puzzling his problem all day—whether to risk taking the
trainees out of the cruisers for harvesting, or
not—and finding Ulla's face intruding on his
thoughts in spite of everything he could do. In
exasperation he had decided that if he could
not solve one problem, at least he would solve
the other—and he headed back toward the
Residence.

As he came in through the Residance front
door onto the soft carpet of the entrance hall,
he heard from beyond the door that led to
Brot's room the soft murmur of voices, one of
them Ulla's.

As he walked toward the door, his boots
noiseless on the carpet, he recognized the other
two voices. One was, of course, Brot's. The
other was the voice of Wilkes. Less than a
pace from the door, Mark checked. For he

could understand now what the voices were saying, and they were talking about him.

"But that's just what I've asked him a number of times," Ulla was saying. "Why?"

"Damn idiot," rumbled Brot's voice.

"No." It was Wilkes speaking. "In a way, it's my fault. I'd never had a pupil like him. And I had no family. I was like a father who dreams about his son following in his footsteps, but being better at it than any man in history. I talked to Mark constantly. I talked too much. I not only filled him up with what he needed to know, but I tried to fill him up with everything I knew, too."

"The hell!" said Brot. "He didn't have to listen, did he? Why wasn't he outside swimming, or skiing, or running around with girls?"

"Because he wasn't an ordinary boy," said Wilkes. "He was a very extraordinary boy—not only because of the mind he had, but because the Meda V'Dan had killed his parents and he'd spent his first thirteen years here with you, Brot."

"What did I do?" growled Brot.

"The same thing I did—only in a different direction," Wilkes said. "I tried to make him all scholar. You tried to make him all outposter. And we both succeeded—too well. With an ordinary boy it might not have done him any harm. But Mark was too capable of learning. He was a finished outposter at thirteen, and a finished scholar at eighteen, and better at being both than either of the men who taught him. You gave him the desire to clean up this colony situation; I gave him the means, the knowledge and theory to work with. From both these things, he's come up with a plan he won't tell us about, except for two things. That it means the end of the Meda V'Dan, and that it means his own end, too, at the hands of the people he'll save from the Meda V'Dan."

"All right," said Brot. "We've got to stop him—that's all."

"Can you stop him from going after the Meda V'Dan?" asked Wilkes.

"Hell, no! How?" exploded Brot.

"Then you can't stop him from going to his own destruction, either," said Wilkes. "They're hooked together, they're both part of a single thing."

"I don't believe it!" broke in Ulla, "I don't! He wouldn't just commit suicide. Not Mark!"

"Suicide? What suicide?" snarled Brot. "He's doing a job where getting it done will get him killed, that's all. And Wilkes's right. He can't do anything. I can't do anything. But you can."

"Me?" There was almost a note of panic in Ulla's voice. "Why do you say it has to be me? He hardly knows I'm here, and you've known him all his life, the two of you together! Why should he listen to me? What can I do you can't do?"

"You know that you can make him want life bad enough, girl," Brot's voice dropped to a rumble. "You're the only one who can do that."

"I?" she said on a strange note. "Then do you

mean, he—"

The chimes of the front door signal sounded through the Residence. Mark turned swiftly and strode softly but rapidly to the door. As he opened it, he heard the door to Brot's room opening behind him. But what else sounded behind him after that he did not hear, for standing on the Residence steps was Orval Belothen, who had captained one of the scout ships that had alternated on watch over the Navy patrol route. Beyond Orval, silver above the browning grass of the landing area, reared his vessel, just returned.

"Meda V'Dan ships, Mark," Orval said. "Six of them. Gathering just at scan limit range beyond the patrol route. And the patrol's due to pass in less than ten hours absolute."

Mark was down the front steps in two long strides and into a ground car.

"Get to the communications building!" he flung over his shoulder at Orval. "Order all cruisers manned and ready to take off as soon as possible."

CHAPTER FIFTEEN

"Lift and go!" said Mark.

They lifted and went—all twelve cruisers and four scout ships. It had taken them over three hours to man the vessels and get them all into space, but the area where the Meda V'Dan were expected to intercept the Navy patrol was less than seven hours away.

They were still one shift from it when both groups—the three mass-forty cruisers of the Navy patrol and the six alien ships, averaging about mass thirty-two—became visible in the scan cubes minutes away from each other.

"They haven't met yet," said Paul, sitting on watch over the scan cube.

"They will," said Mark. "Shift right in on top of them."

The twelve cruisers of Abruzzi Fourteen shifted all together, coming out in a six-point star pattern around both the patrol and the Meda V'Dan vessels. But when they emerged from shift, the conflict they had seen impending when they went into it was already over.

Now, of the three Navy ships, one was literally broken in half. The other two showed gaping cuts and holes in their armour and were drifting out of formation. The alien ships had closed in on them to boarding range, to see what they could pick up in the way of usable equipment.

"Fire at will," said Mark over the intership command circuit.

Filters clamped into place automatically on the view screens as the area enclosed by the Abruzzi Fourteen star pattern was suddenly laced with the soundless but unbearable brilliance of white weapon beams and varicoloured metal explosions. Abruptly, the filters withdrew again, and the six Meda V'Dan ships were revealed, drifting now, torn and broken, while the hull of the cruiser around Mark and his crew pinged and snapped with the sound of cooling weapons.

The air in the cruiser was stiflingly hot and stank of burned insulation. But the fans were clearing and cooling it once more.

"I'm surprised they didn't bring more ships than that—the Meda V'Dan, I mean," said Paul somberly, looking into the nearest screen. He was tight-faced and a little pale with the suddenness of witnessed death.

"They didn't expect us to react this soon, whatever else they expected," answered Mark. His own voice sounded strange in his ears. He bent to the intership command phone.

"Move in and search for survivors," he said. "The Navy ships first."

But there were no survivors. It was part of the ugly business of combat in space with the kind of weapons both sides carried that there were not likely to be survivors, but the search for them was always made. It was made now, and the hold area of Mark's cruiser became a morgue for whatever human bodies could be found, so that they could be returned for burial.

"Now where to?" asked Maura Vols, when the last of these had been brought aboard. Mark had concentrated his most capable people on the ship he had designated flagship for the Abruzzi Fourteen fleet. In theory, any of Maura's pupils could navigate a vessel on his own. In practice, Maura navigated the flagship and her figures were relayed to the other vessels, who followed obediently, although the student navigators were required to calculate on their own so that they could check their results with hers.

"Home?" Paul added. "Or Navy Base?"

"Neither," said Mark. He breathed deeply. He had worked a long time for this moment. Now that it was here, following the instantaneous action of the battle, it felt strange—like an impossible dream suddenly turned into reality. "We'll shift to the Meda V'Dan world, and attack that city of theirs."

There was no response from Paul or Maura. Mark looked up to see them staring at him.

"That's right," Mark said. "That's an order. Get to it."

Maura turned away, and went toward the navigator's section of the command area.

Then Paul turned and went back to his scan cube and communications equipment.

It was three shifts to the edge of the system containing the Meda V'Dan world. On Mark's ship those aboard were generally silent as the shifts were made. It was one thing to practice with ship-mounted weapons; it was something else again to see the results of their use, and the use of other weapons like them. One shift out from the Meda V'Dan world, Mark spoke over the command circuit to the personnel on all twelve ships and four scouts.

"The scouts," he said, "will wait at a distance of one planetary diameter. In case of anything going wrong, they're to head immediately for Abruzzi Station. The cruisers will go in on command together to just over the city and make one slow pass, doing as much damage to the buildings as possible. If there's no return fire, I may order a second pass. If not, all ships—I repeat, all ships—are to get out as quickly as possible. If there's no pursuit, we'll join up together at the edge of this system to return. Otherwise, each vessel will make its own way home. Understood? Ship commanders, acknowledge!"

One by one the ship commanders answered over the command circuit.

"All right," said Mark when they were through. He sat down in his control chair and fastened himself in. "All ships take order and distance from the flagship."

They went in.

There was a heavy cloud cover at three thousand feet over the Meda V'Dan city this day. Their ships broke through this suddenly to see the wide ranks of the identical buildings directly below them.

"Fire at will," said Mark over the command circuit, and the beams of their weapons raked the thin walls of the structures below, sending explosions mounting into the air.

For less than five seconds, they were actually above the city itself. Then their beams stabbed and seared only the slagged rock beyond it, and Mark spoke in the command circuit again.

"Good enough," he said. "Everybody out."

His flagship stood toward space at eight gravities and his head swam. Then they were out at orbit distance, and the sudden, flicking change of a short shift left them at the edge of the Meda V'Dan system.

"Ships!" snapped Paul, his voice suddenly a little hoarse, from where he sat with the communications instruments. "Ships—dozens of them—lifting from the city."

"Get out of here!" said Mark into the command circuit, and heard the words come blurred from between his clamped teeth. "No formation. Each ship home independently. Move!"

He lifted his head from the intership circuit to speak on ship's circuit to Maura.

"Hold shift," he said. "We'll see the rest of them off first."

"Hundreds of ships," said Paul from the scan cube. His voice was no longer hoarse, but there was a numbness to it, as if he were reporting something beyond belief. "Still

coming up from the city. Like bees swarming
. . . the leaders in space already moving fast
our way."

Around the flagship, the other cruisers
were disappearing one by one, like projected
images when the light in the projector is
turned off. There were eleven of them . . .
were nine . . . seven . . . four . . . one . . .

"Ship *Jonas!*" said Mark over the command
circuit at the last ship still hanging there.
"What's wrong?"

There was no answer. Then the *Jonas* also
disappeared.

The air temperature inside the flagship suddenly shot up twenty degrees as a flame
missile from the front ranks of the oncoming
Meda V'Dan exploded only a few hundred
yards short of the cruiser.

"*Shift!*" said Mark to Maura. The alien
ships, the alien system, vanished from the
screen before him and he looked out instead
on the silent and peaceful star scene of four
light-years away.

"Home?" Maura's voice asked him.

"Navy Base," he said.

"Yes, sir," she answered.

He broke the circuit and sat back. After a
second he looked up as a shadow fell across
him. He saw Paul standing over him.

"Navy Base? Now?" asked Paul in a low
voice. "How'll we get out again if they find out
what we've done?"

"I want them to find out," said Mark. "We
won't go all the way in. We'll stop at one of
their approach points and turn the bodies of

the patrol casualties over to it. I think we can do that, tell our story, and get out before those in command at the Base this tour of duty can get ships out to stop us from leaving. And once we're gone, they'll have a chance to think it over, and maybe they'll decide not to do anything until they've consulted Earth."

"You think so?" Paul said.

Mark smiled soberly.

"I'm counting on it," he said.

Nine hours later, their cruiser drifted up to a large, checkerboard-hulled globe, beside which floated a light scout ship like a minnow invisibly tethered to a beach ball.

"Approach point, this is ship *Voltan*," Mark said. Somewhere, a few thousand miles farther on, Navy Base itself was lost in the light of Murgatroyd's Onion. "We are a vessel on Navy lease to Abruzzi Fourteen Station, Garnera Six. Outpost Station Commander Mark Ten Roos speaking. We have cargo to transfer to your approach point station. With your permission, I'll come over and tell you about it while the cargo's being shifted."

"Come ahead, Commander," answered a young voice. "Sub Lieutenant Sharral Ojobki speaking. I'll meet you just inside the lock."

Mark ordered the cruiser into contact range with the globe, and a tubeway was projected from the cruiser air lock to the globe's entrance. A couple of minutes later he passed through that tube, to be met within the air lock of the approach point station by a startlingly tall, lean, and dark young officer.

"Pleasure to have you visit, Commander,"

Ojobki said, shaking hands. "Nothing ever happens on approach point duty. What's the cargo—and can you stop for a drink?"

"I'm afraid not," said Mark. He followed Ojobki's towering figure through the inner air-lock door into the control centre area of the station globe. It was a wide room with walls curving to the angle of the hull overhead, and equipment of all kinds, including communications equipment, against a far wall. There were two Navy enlisted men on duty—one at the communications equipment, the other working at a desk surface with what looked to be station records.

"Too bad," said Ojobki. "The cargo?"

"Bodies," said Mark.

Ojobki stood where he was, looking down at Mark with the welcoming smile still on his face. After a moment, the smile slipped into a baffled frown.

"I'm sorry, sir," he said after a second. "I guess I don't follow you."

"I'm bringing you what I could find of the bodies of your men in the three ships of your Wing Red Four Patrol Unit. They were hit off Domsee by six Meda V'Dan ships." Mark stood aside as two of his colonist crew came through the air lock behind him, carrying the first of the frozen, blanket-wrapped bodies.

"Lay them down over there by the wall," Mark said.

The colonists obeyed, setting their burden down gently and then going back out past another two who had just entered with another blanket-wrapped burden.

"I—" Ojobki broke off. He stepped over and began to unwrap the blanket from the front end of the object. The crewmen slowed, hesitated, and glanced at Mark.

"Let him look," said Mark.

The two men stood still. Ojobki threw back a flap of the blanket and looked. His face twisted. He carefully rewrapped the blanket and stepped back from the body. At a nod from Mark the two took it on to lay it down beside the first one that had been brought in.

Ojobki's throat worked. He turned to Mark.

"I don't understand," he said to Mark. His voice was unsteady, shaky at first, but grew firmer. "You say the Meda V'Dan did *this?*" He shook his head like a man trying to get rid of the effects of a blow.

"I've got to report this—" He started to turn toward the communications equipment, then froze as the side arm Mark was wearing appeared abruptly in Mark's hand.

"Not just yet," said Mark. He gestured with the weapon at the Navy enlisted man sitting at the equipment. "All right. Move away from there."

The enlisted man stared. Slowly he got to his feet and backed away from the equipment.

"Good enough," said Mark. "Stand still."

He turned back to Ojobki.

"I can't take any chances on being held up now," he said. "I've got to get back to Abruzzi Fourteen Station. After we smashed the six Meda V'Dan vessels that hit your patrol, my ships and I went on to the one Meda V'Dan world we know about, and hit their city to pay them back. I'd warned the aliens not to touch Navy ships."

Ojobki stared back at him as if Mark were talking some strange foreign tongue.

"Here," said Mark. He reached into a pocket with his free hand and came out with a small grey spool of wire, which he dropped on the top of a nearby instrument. "There's a copy of the record of our fight with the six alien ships and our pass over their city."

He glanced over at the two men currently carrying in a body. There was a long row of the silent objects now, on the other side of the room.

"How many more?" Mark asked.

"This is the last one," said the colonist in the lead.

"All right," said Mark. He waited until the two set their burden down and headed back out the lock. Then he backed toward the lock himself, keeping Ojobki and the two enlisted men covered. "You can notify your superiors as soon as I go. Tell them, though, that no matter what the Navy does, we're going to stay where we are and defend our colony."

He backed out through the open inner air-lock door, and turning, sprinted through the tube back into the cruiser.

"Pull tube," he said to Paul, as soon as he was back inside his own ship. "Home to Abruzzi Fourteen."

Back at Abruzzi Fourteen, they found all the other eleven cruisers and four scouts safely returned before them. Mark nodded, and called a meeting at the Residence of all the station outposters, together with Jarl, Ulla, Wilkes, Lily, Maura and the new factory production head, Age Hammerschold.

"I want a continual watch kept by one of the scouts on Navy Base," he told them. "Unless I've been dead wrong from the start, most of the Navy, or maybe all of it, is going to be abandoning the Base in the next week or so. And Brot, now's the time to get together here those outposters I had you make a list of. The ones we can work with, because from here on it's a job for all the Stations and all the Colonies. We're going to sink or swim together."

CHAPTER SIXTEEN

It took twelve days before the outposters on
Brot's list could all be notified and gathered
in from the half-dozen Colony Worlds spread
out through three different solar systems, for
most of them had nothing but ground transportation available to them—the Navy having
always taken care of movement between
worlds and stars.

Consequently, the sixteen ships of Abruzzi
Station Fourteen became busy acting as
transports. Meanwhile, what Mark had predicted came true. The Navy precipitously
abandoned Navy Base, without even leaving
caretakers behind, and pulled back to Earth.
But four days later, from Earth to Abruzzi
Fourteen came a single tough heavily-armed
little ship. Emblazoned on its hull was the
black outposter seal of a gauntleted hand cup-
ping a star in its palm.

It landed without hesitation directly under
the fixed plasma rifles Mark had ordered set
up to cover the landing area, and two compe-

tent-looking men in outposter uniform but with colonel's insignia on their shoulders exited from the ship and demanded to be taken to Mark.

They were brought to him in the library of the Residence, where he sat behind a desk laden with unfinished paperwork.

"Gentlemen," he said, getting to his feet as they were ushered in. "Sit down."

"This isn't a social call, Commander," said the older of the two. "You're under arrest. We're here to take you back to Earth to stand charges of genocide and incitement of aliens to genocide."

"I'm sorry," Mark shook his head. "But I'm not going anywhere right away. And for that matter, neither are you." He nodded at the door behind them, and the two ranking Outposter Headquarters officers turned around to see a couple of young colonists holding plasma rifles aimed at them.

"You're under arrest yourselves," said Mark. "Take their side arms." He watched as the colonels were relieved of the hand weapons each wore in regulation outposter fashion. "And now, you might as well sit down."

He himself sat and nodded to the two colonists, who withdrew, taking the officers' guns with them.

Neither colonel moved toward a chair, however. The older of the two, a tall, spare man with thinning grey hair, black eyebrows, and a narrow jaw, stared hard at Mark.

"You're resisting your own superior officers?" he said.

"Not anymore," said Mark. "Abruzzi Station Fourteen is an independent colony now, and all of us here who were outposters have emigrated to it and become colonists."

"Colonists!" said the older colonel. "Revolutionists—that's what you are. Every man sent out to the Outposts is sworn to protect human life, and you not only haven't done that, you've stirred up the aliens to attack Earth." His mouth was a pinched slit. "What're you going to do with us, then? Shoot us?"

"Just keep you quiet for a while until I can take you for a short trip," said Mark. "Then I'll send you back to Earth to tell them what you saw."

"While you run the other way?"

Mark shook his head.

"I'll be coming to Earth, too," he said. "Just as soon as I've got things wound up here. But meanwhile"—he reached out and spoke into his desk communicator. "You can come and show the officers to their quarters now," he said into the instrument.

The two armed colonists reappeared and ushered the colonels out. Mark spoke into the communicator.

"Prepare the flagship for immediate lift-off on a twenty-hour cruise," he said.

Five minutes later, Mark's work was again interrupted by another visitor. This time it was Ulla.

"You aren't going back to Earth with them?" Ulla said without preamble. Her face was pale.

Mark hesitated.

"No," he said. "Sit down?"

"You're sure?"

He smiled.

"What's wrong with me today?" he said. "No one wants to sit down when I ask them to. Those officers wouldn't, and now you won't."

He reached over and turned the chair by the side of his desk a little toward her.

"Sit down," he said. She came and sat, but stiffly upright in the chair. "Tell me how you happened to find out those officers were in here to take me back."

"Don't you think I've been expecting someone like that?" she said. "Don't you think all of us have? You let us know you expected something like this right from the start, and then these men come. What else are we supposed to think, but that you're going back with them to stand trial?"

"I see. You've talked to them," Mark said, watching her closely.

"To them first." She stared unflinchingly at him. "Then I came to you. But you promise me you're not going to let them take you back?"

"I promise," he said.

She looked at him suspiciously. For a long couple of seconds they watched each other without words, and then something began to move between them that did not need words. Abruptly Mark got to his feet, picked up some papers, and put them away in a file drawer so that he turned away from her. When he turned back and sat down again, his face was settled.

"Now you've made up your mind," she said.

"I'm always making up my mind," he said lightly.

"Stop it!" she said. "Don't play words with me. You know what I mean. You've reached that point in your plans where you always thought you'd go and throw your life away to make sure what you started kept going. Maybe for some reason you aren't actually going back with those two, but some way or another you're planning on giving yourself up to the crowd back on Earth for execution."

He sobered.

"And you're here to save me, is that it?" he said.

"I can't save you against your will if that's what you mean," she said. "The others think I can, but I know better. All I can do is ask you to save yourself."

He shook his head.

"Don't do that," she said. "You act like you hate people, but you really love them—and we all know it. You love them so much you're prepared to believe the worst about them and go right on working to make life better for them, even though you expect them to kill you for it. But you're part of people, too. Why can't you love yourself enough to save yourself from the rest of them?"

He shook his head again, this time with finality.

"Lions have teeth," he said, "and they can't help using them. That's lion nature. Take a thorn out of the paw of one of them and in spite of the folk tales he's not likely to lick your face." He smiled a little. "The human race always turns on the man who makes it live—and pays its debt by getting rid of him. The war leader gets tossed into the rubbish heap in peacetime; the man of peace is crucified once fighting starts."

He stopped speaking. He had not meant to say so much, and he was a little startled to hear the words pour out. But, looking across the corner of his desk at her, he saw that even with this he had not convinced her.

"I'm sorry, Ulla," he said more gently. "But it comes down to this—there's a physics to human events, and one of the natural laws of that physics is that if you do a good deed, you've got to pay for having done it. You don't understand this, Brot doesn't understand it, Wilkes doesn't understand—but that doesn't change anything. The law goes right on working, just the same, and there's nothing I can do about it."

She got to her feet. Her eyes were hard.

"I don't believe you!" she said. "All right, maybe there are laws like that. But I don't believe a man who could figure out how to change history can't figure out how to save himself, once the change is made. I just don't believe it! The trouble with you, Mark, is you've made yourself face the possibility people could turn on you for so long that you've forgotten it's only a possibility, not a certainty. Now you're going to lie down and die when you don't have to, rather than admit you don't have to!"

She turned and went to the door. With her

hand on the latch button, she turned around again.

"I can't make you change," she said. "But I can do one thing. I can make sure whatever you let them do to you, they do to me, too! Try that on your conscience about people! If you let them destroy you, now, you'll be letting them destroy someone else as well—someone who didn't even do your good deed for them!"

She went out.

He sat where he was for a little time without moving. Then, slowly, he went back to his paperwork.

A little over two hours later, his desk communicator buzzed.

"Yes?" he said.

"Flagship crewed and ready for lift-off on twenty-hour cruise as ordered," the voice of Paul answered.

"Good," said Mark. "I'll be right there."

He broke connection on that call and made another.

"Bring those outposter colonels back here," he said into the communicator. "And get us a couple of ground cars. Tell them I'm taking them for a short trip."

He took the two to board the flagship by a circular route that hid their boarding from the small ship that had carried them from Earth. Five minutes after they were all on board, the flagship lifted off.

"Where are you taking us?" the older colonel asked once they were in orbit.

"Colonel—" Mark began, and broke off. "I don't know your name."

"Branuss," said the colonel stiffly. He nodded at his companion. "Colonel Ubi."

"All right, gentlemen," said Mark. "To answer the question, I'm not going to take you anywhere. I'm going to let your ship take us someplace. Colonel Branuss, will you be good enough to get on the communications, there, and talk to your ship back at Abruzzi Fourteen? Tell them to lift off and join us here, and also, Colonel—"

Branuss, halfway to the communications equipment, stopped and turned.

"Remind them that they may be a very good ship, but that this cruiser has the armament to turn them into junk in two minutes—and at any attempt by them to do anything but follow orders, we'll open fire."

Branuss turned sharply on his heel and went on the communications equipment. Mark heard him relaying both the directions and the warning to the ship on the planet's surface below.

The ship from Earth had been standing by ready for an emergency lift-off at any minute; but the lift-off they had been ordered to make was not an emergency. It took them nearly an hour to run a routine countdown check and nearly another hour to come alongside the cruiser in orbit.

"Now," said Mark to Branuss, who was back at the communications equipment and waiting. "They know where the world is that holds the Meda V'Dan city we hit some days ago to start all this. Tell them to navigate both ships there. They navigate and give us the fig-

ures. We'll follow. That's so you won't have
any doubt you've been to the right place afterward. And tell them, too, I've arranged to have
three other cruisers follow one shift behind. If
they try to duck away from us by shifting
someplace else while we make an oncourse
shift, the following vessels will spot them in
their scan cubes and hunt them down."

"That's not necessary," said Branuss tight-
ly. "If I order our ship to go to a particular
destination, it'll go there."

"Good," said Mark. "But those three
cruisers will still be following, just in case.
We'll be calculating our own navigation on
this ship too, just in case they think to navigate to somewhere else than the Meda V'Dan
world."

Branuss relayed the orders.

Five shifts in a direct line from Garnera
system to the system containing the Meda
V'Dan world brought them to orbit around it.
The two colonels watched the view screens
tensely as the alien world appeared upon it.
For a few seconds they stared at it; then
Branuss swung about to face Mark, who was
standing a few feet away.

"No ships," he said.

His voice was tight, and his face was not
exactly pale, but its features were set hard.

"You didn't think we'd get this far and live,
did you?" asked Mark.

He waited for an answer.

"No," said Branuss grudgingly.

"No," said Mark. "And now we have. And
now, for the first time, it begins to occur to

me that the reaction of the Meda V'Dan to my raid on their city may not have been exactly what the Navy and the Earth government assumed it would be. Isn't that right?"

Again he waited.

"Possibly," said Branuss, as if the word were a part of him that had to be amputated before it could be uttered.

"Possibly," echoed Mark gently. "Shall we go down to the city itself, then?"

He had to repeat the question before Branuss turned to the communications equipment and ordered the smaller ship to lead them down to the location of the alien city.

Once again, as on the day of the raid by the Abruzzi Fourteen cruisers, there was a cloud cover only a few thousand feet above the city site. The smaller ship from Earth gave the cruiser the coordinates for approach, and together, the two vessels descended, until they broke through the thick white layer of the cloud-stuff to emerge into the grey day below above the bare plain and the slagged rock that encircled the city site.

The two ships, having emerged over location, hung still, and their viewers looked down to show on screens what was beneath. For a long moment in the cruiser there was silence as everyone—not just the two colonels from Earth—looked.

Then Branuss turned his head sideways to look at Mark, and spoke. "There's nothing there," he said.

Mark nodded, at him and at the screen which showed five square miles of bare, scarred bedrock littered with metal and other junk, as if some monster picnic had been held and abandoned there.

"That's right," Mark said. "They're gone. They're gone for good. There isn't a Meda V'Dan within light-years of this world, or Earth—and there never will be again."

CHAPTER SEVENTEEN

When the two ships landed again back at Abruzzi Fourteen, Mark escorted the two colonels over to their own vessel.

"Here," he said, as they parted at the fore air lock of the smaller ship. He handed Branuss two grey wire spools and a black report tape.

"These greys," he said, "are copies of our recorded action with the Meda V'Dan following their attack on the Navy patrol and our raid on their city. The black tape report spool has a message from us to the Earth-City government, explaining why we acted the way we did, and why the Meda V'Dan moved out. It also offers an agreement to the Earth-City by which it and we, the Independent Colonies, can both benefit from our new relationship. I'll expect a favourable answer to the general points in the agreement in ten days. If we haven't got it by that time, we'll assume the reaction of Earth-City government is negative, and go ahead with plans that don't include

Earth."

Branuss took the spools without question. There was about him something of the same air of dazed belief and automatic obedience that had characterized the colonists Mark had seen loading aboard the *Wombat* on his way to Abruzzi Fourteen, months earlier.

"They can't answer in ten days," the colonel muttered. "That's impossible."

"So was the Meda V'Dan situation out here," said Mark. "Now it's not impossible. Ten days. Good-bye, gentlemen."

He watched them board, and the small ship seal and lift. Then he went back to the Residence. But he was barely once more immersed in his mass of paperwork when he found himself invaded by Brot, Wilkes, Ulla, and Lily, all together.

"The Meda V'Dan have gone?" demanded Brot as soon as the group was inside the library door. "And you knew they'd go? Why'n hell didn't you tell the rest of us?"

Mark leaned back in his chair and wearily rubbed the inside corners of his eyes.

"I didn't know," he said. "I only guessed they would. I bet on it, in fact. But the bet paid off."

"If you were guessing that far ahead," said Lily, "why did you need me digging into the Meda V'Dan philosophy and character? I never guessed they could be scared out just by a few ships attacking their city. Particularly a city where they must have had thousands of their own vessels and weapons, and everything else. I still can't believe it."

"They weren't scared out," said Mark.

"No," said Wilkes thoughtfully, "I see what you mean. They went because that's their behaviour pattern. But what Lily asks is a good question, and I'd like to ask it, too. You didn't need me, or her, after all? Then why did you just pretend to give us work to do? I thought" —his voice was a little husky—"I really thought I was being useful to you."

"You were," said Mark. "So was Lily. You ought to know me better than that. I was out to get rid of the aliens. But we had to learn as much about them as possible before we lost them, because we're going to have to know as much as we can when we start trying to deal firsthand with the Unknown Races, further in toward the galaxy's centre. You and Lily, and her assistants, have been putting together what we have to know to make the Independent Colonies work."

"So, now *we're* going to trade with the aliens farther in?" Brot demanded. "You planned that from the start too?"

"If we got rid of the Meda V'Dan, yes," said Mark. "There's a market on Earth for alien goods, and plainly there's a market among the Unknown Races somewhere for human goods, or it wouldn't have been worth the time of the Meda V'Dan to steal from us, or trade with us for what they couldn't use themselves. We can take those markets over to pay for the things from Earth-City we'll still need, until we get heavy manufacturing and other industry set up out here."

"All right—" began Brot.

"Forgive me," said Mark, "but this is something I'd rather not go into now. I'll be bringing it all out at the meeting with the other outposters in just a few days, now. Can you wait until then? I've got"—he waved at the desk—"more than I can do here between then and now as it is, and once I start explaining, it won't be easy to stop. There are certain things that have to be done before that meeting, no matter what else happens."

He stopped talking. They looked at him. Then Brot grunted and swung his power chair around. Following him silently, everyone but Ulla turned and went out.

"I'm afraid," said Mark to her, looking at the door that had closed behind the other three, "I've made everybody think I didn't trust them."

"No," said Ulla. "They'll understand. But give them a little while to get used to the Meda V'Dan being gone. It's a big thing, you know, and no one else expected it the way you did."

"No," said Mark. "That's true."

"I'll talk to them," she said, and left him.

He returned to the unrelenting pressure of the work on the desk before him.

Four days later, the last of the other Outpost commanders invited to the meeting had been gathered from their various worlds and stations. There were one hundred and forty-three of them, one for each of the active Colonies that had been guarded by Navy Base. They met in the auditorium of Abruzzi Fourteen's Section One village.

Up on the stage at one end, Mark sat in the

centre of a long table facing the audience, with Brot and the other station outposters to his right, and Wilkes, Lily, Jarl, Maura Vols, and Age Hammerschold to his left. A voice pickup overhead carried their voices from the stage to the far end of the auditorium, and other pickups out over the heads of the audience waited to air the questions or comments from the floor.

"Before we invited you here," said Mark without preamble, as soon as Brot had introduced him, "you knew our Abruzzi Fourteen ships had smashed a gang of Meda V'Dan vessels that cut up a Navy patrol, and that we'd gone on to hit the Meda V'Dan city. I take it there's no one here who thinks our action wasn't justified?"

There was a mutter quickly rising to a growl of approval from the audience and a burst of hard, brief applause.

"All right," said Mark, "since then, up until this moment, you've heard that the Navy has abandoned Navy Base and pulled back to Earth, that Abruzzi Fourteen has declared its status as an Independent Colony, and that a few days ago I went to the Meda V'Dan city with a couple of outposter senior officers from Earth who were here to arrest me and we found the Meda V'Dan city was gone."

Another burst of applause, brief but thunderous.

"All right," said Mark. "Then you're all pretty well briefed on the situation as it stands right now. Abruzzi Fourteen's gone ahead and declared its independence, and we're going to stick to that. The rest of you can do what you want, of course, but to put it bluntly, what's needed right now is for all of us to go independent together and form a community of colonies that can react as a group—toward Earth or any of the Unknown Races we run across. In fact, I've sent what amounts to an ultimatum to the Earth-City, tailored to the idea that we're all going to be united eventually in independence. You've all been handed copies of that message, and I suppose most of you've had a chance to read it by now. But to save time here, suppose I run over the important points of it."

He paused and reached for a typescript that was lying on the table in front of him.

"There are two parts to it," he said. "The first is an explanation of what happened, and why the Meda V'Dan left. This explanation isn't just guesswork. It's a series of conclusions drawn about the Meda V'Dan character by Abruzzi Fourteen's team of experts, who are here this evening." He nodded to his left. "Mr. Wilkes Danielson, one of the Earth-City's foremost anthropologists, and just beyond him, Miss Lily Betaugh, one of our colonists who was formerly a full professor at the University of Belgrade. Mr. Danielson is responsible for the theory about the Meda V'Dan character on which the research of Miss Betaugh and her staff was based."

He broke off.

"While I'm at it," he said, "I'd better introduce the rest of our colony's experts. Just beyond Miss Betaugh is Jarl Rakkal—you probably recognize the name from banking matters back in the Earth-City—who's set up a highly successful economic system, not only for this colony, but potentially for all our Colonies in association if and when we reach that point. Mr. Rakkal's come up with trade goods that interested the Meda V'Dan for trade with the Unknown Races and should undoubtedly interest the Unknown Races themselves. Mrs. Maura Vols, just beyond, has been our lead navigation and positions officer and also head of our school for student navigators—a school we plan to expand into all areas of ship handling, under her direction. At the end is Mr. Age Hammerschold, our factory executive."

He turned to his right.

"And, of course," he said, "you all know or know of Brot Halliday, whom we've got to thank for organizing the watch on the Navy patrols and for the success of our encounter with the Meda V'Dan in space and at their city—"

"What the bloody hell?" snarled Brot under his breath. "Why are you trying to put off all the credit onto somebody else? Why?"

"Thanks to all these people, and not forgetting the other outposters at Abruzzi Fourteen"—and Mark nodded to his right at Race, Paul, Orval, and an outposter named Soone who had finally filled the vacancy left by Stein—"I was able to put together the half of the message that explains the Meda V'Dan leaving and tells Earth what we want from them, and what we can give them in exchange."

He shuffled the typescript, glanced over a

page, and cleared his throat.

"Briefly," he said, "and you can read the details later—we were able to get rid of the Meda V'Dan because they lacked a modern civilization, in our terms. To quote from the message: *The work of Mr. Danielson and Miss Betaugh indicated that these aliens actually had been frozen in a very primitive cultural pattern, to which they attributed their survival as a race, and to which, therefore, they would adhere undeviatingly as long as there was an alternative course of action that permitted continuing adherence.*"

Mark ceased reading and looked up from the page to the audience.

"What she means," he said, "is that the Meda V'Dan would do anything rather than change their ways because they believed that they'd go on surviving as a race only as long as they didn't change. In fact, they told us, when we visited their city earlier, that they'd been around before all other races were born, and they'd still be around when all other races were dead."

He paused a second to let that sink in to the audience.

"That bit of talk," he said, "was our first evidence that the work done by Mr. Danielson and Miss Betaugh was on the right track. By sheer chance on that same visit I was lucky enough to get down into the lower part of one of their city buildings and see that the bottom levels were taken up by large power units. In short, each one of their buildings was an oversized spaceship with room inside to hold their smaller ships and everything else they wanted to carry about."

He paused again, and Wilkes spoke up quickly.

"Commander Ten Roos," Wilkes said, "is being unduly modest about this whole matter of interpreting the Meda V'Dan character—"

Mark put a hand gently on the older man's shoulder to interrupt him.

"That's all right," he said to Wilkes, the pickups overhead carrying his words to the far end of the auditorium, "these aren't Earth-City representatives. We can tell them the truth. In fact, they need to know the truth so they can get a clear picture of the situation. The fact is, I wasn't much more than a focal point for all this. I couldn't have done any of it without these specialists and experts you see here at the table. But, to get back to the Meda V'Dan and why they left—"

He took his hand from Wilkes's shoulder, and the older man sat back, silent. Mark went on.

"It has to be pretty much guesswork as to how they started into space," he said. "Chances are they were contacted by some interstellar-travelling race when they were still in the culture stage we saw them in now. Somehow, they got hold of ships themselves, and simply transplanted that culture into space. What they are, essentially, is a nomad culture which carries all its belongings with it as it travels and doesn't so much inhabit the worlds it stops on, as camp there."

He broke off.

"Take a look at page eight of the type-script," he said. "Our estimate of their culture is set down in detail there—" There was a rustling of pages throughout the audience as his listeners went to the page he had mentioned. "Briefly, the Meda V'Dan live by trading if they have to, but prefer to steal if they can because it's easier. Whenever they run across another race they can steal from profitably, they camp in the vicinity and take as much as they can for as long as they can. When the other race starts getting after them for stealing, they simply pack up and go else-where—not because they don't have the equipment and the technology to stand and fight back, but because they're committed to their nomad existence and it's simply more profitable to go find another victim race than to stay and argue the point."

Mark turned several pages of his own tran-script and laid it flat before him.

"That's the sum of it, then," he said. "Indi-cations are the Meda V'Dan never were able to tell one of us from another—just as they all looked alike to us—and they no more under-stood our culture and ways than we did theirs. But there was something else in their case. They didn't care whether they under-stood or not, and consequently when this one colony hit their home base with a handful of ships, they assumed the human race as a whole was fed up with them—and left."

He paused.

"Now, look at the final section that begins on page twenty-three," he said. "This is the short agreement I sent back to Earth for the government there to accept or refuse. But I think they'll accept, since they've got nothing to lose but some military hardware they don't need anyway, and a dumping ground for their excess population, which they'd have to find some other way of curbing, in any case. What the agreement asks is that they give up Navy Base, with all its equipment, supplies, and ships that have been left behind, to the Colonies, that shipments of colonists cease immediately, newcomers from Earth being welcome out here only as voluntary immigrants who have been accepted by some particular colony. We should be able to pick up just the sort of professional and trained people we want by sifting those who do want to emigrate out here voluntarily. Finally, they can also cease shipments of supplies to the Colonies— that's something they'd do anyway—and any trade with the Unknown Races must be channelled through us."

Mark pushed the typescript from him.

"There you've got it," he told the audience. "We may be a little pinched for home-grown vegetables for a winter season or two on our various worlds. But there are good enough food stocks stored in Navy Base to see that none of our Colonies goes hungry for several years. Meanwhile, we can be training people to handle the Navy ships and we can start almost immediately sending exploratory vessels in toward Galactic Centre to contact the Unknown Races for trading purposes. We've got pretty good evidence the UR aren't likely to be either inimical or uncooperative, otherwise the Meda V'Dan would have been wiped out long ago."

He paused and looked slowly from front to back over the whole audience.

"All right," he said. "There it is. Now, what Abruzzi Fourteen would like from all of you assembled here would be a vote of confidence. How about it? Will you give us your vote?"

There was a silence lasting several seconds, then a lean, middle-aged outposter in the third row got to his feet.

"I'm Commander Murta Vey, Thanought Nine Station, Alameda Two," he said. "Generally speaking, I've liked what I heard. But I've got a question—why didn't you let the rest of us know what you were doing here before this? It seems to me we had a stake in it as well as you . . ."

The talk began. It ran back and forth between audience and stage for nearly two hours before Brot slammed his wide palm on the table in front of him and shouted everyone else down.

"God damn it!" he roared. "Are we going to sit here all night? The Meda V'Dan are gone. The thing's done, isn't it?"

He waited. After a second there was a rumble of agreement, drowned out by applause.

"All right!" shouted Brot. "And now that it's done, you like it better this way than it was before, with the Navy sitting there doing nothing and more half-collapsed colonists being dumped on each of us at least twice a year, and the aliens shooting us up every so often—don't you?"

This time the applause was louder and more prolonged.

"Then what're we waiting for?" demanded Brot. "Let's take a vote, damn it, and end this business!"

The applause this time was overwhelming. Brot slumped back in his power chair, grunting with satisfaction and waving at Mark with his one hand.

"Take over," he said.

"All right," said Mark, and his voice carried via the pickups out over the last of the applause. "Let's vote by getting up and leaving, all who're in favor of what Abruzzi Fourteen's done, and the agreement we sent Earth. Those who don't agree can stay here and make their own plans accordingly."

He got to his feet. The others on stage rose behind him, all but Brot, who turned his power chair away from the table. Down on the auditorium floor, the audience was already on its feet and pouring into the aisles.

By the time Mark and the others from Abruzzi Fourteen reached the floor in front of the stage, those aisles were full. Slowly they followed the last to leave, and as they left the auditorium by its far doors, Mark turned around and looked back.

Less than a dozen figures still stood in a ragged group down by the front rows of the now-empty seats, their ranks stretching the length of the building.

The audience spilled out onto the grass and

pavement of the Section One village, dark figures in clumps and groups, still talking under the newly risen moon of Garnera VI. They moved generally toward the village's original community mess hall—now a gym and sports centre—where food and drink had been laid out. Mark went with the rest, and spent half an hour moving around and speaking to people at the mess hall; then he slipped out quietly by himself and returned by ground car to the Residence.

In the Residence library, his desk was at last cleared of paper. He went around behind it and opened one of its drawers to take out a folder containing some thirty sheets of handwritten paper. In ink on the front of the folder was a brief note in the handwriting of Maura Vols.

"Basic pattern for ten-shift navigation, Garnera VI to Earth—Property of M. Vols: DO NOT REMOVE FROM FILES!"

He laid the folder on the desk and sat down to the dictagraph to do a short message, which he folded, put in an unsealed envelope, and left lying on his desk. Taking the folder, he went to his room, where he packed a small luggage case.

With luggage case and folder, he went once more back out into the night and down to the landing area before the Residence. The colonist on duty there did not see him pass, and a few moments later Mark quietly activated the outside controls for the air-lock entrance to one of the heavy scout ships and went in, closing the air lock behind him.

The scouts, like all the Abruzzi Fourteen ships, were currently on standby ready. He needed only to run the check list and heat the engine and operating equipment. Then the scout was ready to lift, except for a final obstruction check of its takeoff area.

Quietly, with the lights in the scout off behind him, Mark opened the lock and stepped out. He made one circuit of the ship, confirming the fact that there was nothing in the way of her lift-off, and he was just about to re-enter the lock when a voice spoke behind him.

"To Earth?"

Mark turned. Brot floated in his power chair a few feet away, his face obscured in the shadow of the scout's hull.

"Yes," said Mark.

For a moment Brot said nothing.

"It's a damn thing," he said then, "a damn thing, you throwing your life away like this."

Mark took a step toward him.

"Dad," he said, "you've got to understand. Earth's going to have to save face. We've got to throw them some kind of bone."

"The hell we do," said Brot. "You said it yourself—they're better off without the Colonies and without supporting a Navy out here. What more do they have to have, icing on their cake?"

"Yes," said Mark. "Common sense only takes care of part of it. There's another part —the fact that specific people in Earth-City government have been wrong about the Meda V'Dan all these years, putting up with the aliens raiding and stealing when now it turns out any kind of firm action would have put an end to that. They're going to get jumped on by the mass of voters back on Earth, and they'll want a scapegoat, someone to divert attention. If I don't give them one on their front doorstep, they'll come out here to dig one up before they give in, and that could end up wrecking everything. In five years, even, we'll be able to handle the Navy ships, and we'll probably have made contact with the Unknown Races, to say nothing of having gotten all our Colonies self-supporting. But right now none of that's done, yet. We need time to train spacemen, we need the stored food at Navy Base—and Earth government needs an excuse to give in gracefully. They can blame me for everything everyone back there doesn't like, and take credit themselves for the good points. They have to have that.''

"No," said Brot. He was hunched in the power chair like an old bear growling in a cave mouth.

"I'm sorry," said Mark. He backed up against the air-lock door and reached for its outside control without taking his eyes off Brot.

"I'll go with you," said Brot.

"Now, that would be a waste," said Mark. He felt the outer air-lock door move in away from his fingers, opening.

"They'd make a scapegoat out of anyone who was with me, too, and one's all they need." He shook his head. "No, I'll go alone."

"Fake it," said Brot. "There are mountains back a few hundred miles from here where you could hide a scout like that for a hundred years. Remember that canyon with the waterfall where I took you hunting on your twelfth birthday? Ditch that ship there, and I'll come get you two nights from now.''

Mark shook his head.

"No," he said. "Brot . . . Dad, I'm sorry. But I've got to do this. I'm right about the way they'd act back on Earth if I didn't."

"You're damn wrong," said Brot. "You think ordinary men've got guts like you? You've already knocked them down. They're not going to get up just to be knocked down again."

"I'm sorry," said Mark. "I'm sorry, but there's only one way to do this so nobody but me gets hurt. Good-bye . . .''

He stepped quickly back into the air-lock, punching the button that opened the inner lock door and closed the outer one. He had been afraid for his strength of will if Brot had talked even a little more, but the door closed without the older man saying another word.

He turned on the lights inside the scout and went quickly to the control area. He was eager now to get on his way. He sat down in the command chair and initiated the lift-off procedure. For a moment he had a fleeting worry about the closeness of Brot to the ship. But Brot was too old a hand not to have moved back a safe distance.

To make sure, however, he flipped his viewing screens on heat response and made a quick scan of the immediate area. There was no human body within fifty yards of him. He lifted ship.

The scout went up with a smooth roar, which whispered out into silence as he left the atmosphere behind and the engines switched automatically to tail chambers. His viewing screens now showed the night side of Garnera VI, black below him. He drove out to a safe distance, switched drive units, and programmed for the first shift toward Earth, working from the figures in Maura Vols's folder.

He shifted.

Abruptly the screens were bright with a different view of stars. He sat for a moment, watching them, then reached for the folder a little wearily and began to compare the figures in it for the second shift with the automatic position reckoning as the ship's computers were already building it in on the plot screen before him. It was a purely reflexive reaction, born of the old familiar habit he had cultivated to guard himself at all times against the mistakes of others. Maura Vols did not make mistakes—particularly where the course she dealt with was from Garnera to Earth . . .

He checked. There was a figure in Maura's calculations that had been erased and changed. There should be nothing in that fact alone, but there was something about the figure as it stood now that bothered him, amateur navigator that he was. He went to the wide margin of the paper, filled with Maura's own figurings.

The calculations for the figure he had just read were there. They, too, had been erased and changed. He sat down to check them by his own slow calculations.

It took him less than ten minutes to find what he sought. The new figure Maura had set down was not only a fractional but a retrograde figure. Not only was it incorrect for an Earth destination, but followed out it gave him anything but the first jump toward the solar system he had intended. Instead of being three light-years from his starting point, he was now two Garnera-system diameters *farther away* from Earth than he had been to begin with. Not only that, but he happened to be in exactly the position that would make possible an easy, invisible return to that same mountainous part of Garnera VI which Brot had suggested to him as a hiding place.

He threw his stylus down in disgust. He could, of course, attempt the task of navigating himself to Earth. But, starting from this present, unfamiliar point in space, his chances of losing his way forever among the stars were easily a thousand to one. He was simply too inexperienced a navigator.

There was a faint sound behind him in the ship. He hesitated, feeling a presence, like a faint pressure on the short hairs at the nape of his neck. Slowly, he turned and looked.

In the entrance leading from the cabin level to the pilot room of the ship Ulla was standing gazing back at him. She continued to stand there, even after he had turned to face her.

"Now you know," she said. "You belong to others beside yourself. Did you think we'd ever let you rob us of yourself, with so much yet to be done?"

CHAPTER EIGHTEEN

"They require guarantees," said Jarl. "Guarantees we'll profit from the trades, and penalty payments if the guarantees aren't met."

It was nearly six months since the meeting that had gathered outposters from all the Colonies at Abruzzi Fourteen. It was therefore almost six months since Mark and Ulla had lifted from Garnera VI in the scout ship. The recently elected Governing Board for Abruzzi Fourteen Colony was gathered to decide a matter of some conflict with the government of Earth, concerning the use of some of the equipment formerly belonging to Navy Base as direct trade goods with one of the three Unknown Races so far contacted by the colonists. They had met in the library of the former Residence, now the colony headquarters building, and there were only two outposters present—Paul and Brot. Otherwise, the Abruzzi Fourteen voters had elected colonists like themselves to govern them—Jarl,

Lily, Maura Vols, and Age Hammerschold. Wilkes Danielson would have been elected also, but he was upstairs now, dying, in the last stages of bone cancer.

Brot sat at the far end of the table by a window, his opinion little in demand at the gathering, and with no great interest in giving it. All his attention was on the landing area. It was spring at Garnera VI, and the first ship-load of trading-station personnel and recolonists were loading for a destination down-galaxy, to set up a post on an uninhabited world not five light-years from one of the Unknown Races. One of the cruisers was waiting, and already most of those to go with her to that destination were aboard. For weeks now Abruzzi Fourteen had swarmed with strange colonists and outposters from other stations as these were sifted for those best qualified to plant this new, farther colony. Brot, almost a supernumerary nowadays, had volunteered for the task of certifying those finally chosen.

Now at least that part of the job was done, and his dark eyes were fixed tensely out the window, as he observed the last-minute actions about the cruiser, preparatory to its departure. So far, those for whom he watched had not arrived.

"What's the point?" muttered Age. "They've already given the stuff up to us. What difference does it make to Earth-City government whether we use it or trade it to the Amnhohen?"

"None," said Jarl. "But it's a chance for

them to twist our arms and hold us up for better terms. You've got to get that straight, Age. They'll hit us any time they get the chance. In this case, they're going back to the old business about Mark.''

"What do they want us to do?'' snapped Age. "Stop everything else and spend the next ten thousand years trying to find his body?''

Outside, as Brot watched, the main entrance to the cruiser was closed and sealed, leaving only the ladder to the open fore lock available for last-minute cargo and personnel. The colony spacemen on guard at the lock had now moved out to a safe distance and were checking last-minute items and crew aboard from the perimeter. The new grass of spring was dark about the underside of the checkerboard hull.

"Not really,'' said Jarl. "It's just a means of advancing a claim. Remember, the agreement Mark started to make with them was never actually signed.''

"We're acting as though it was,'' said Lily. "So are they.''

"That's right,'' said Jarl, with a slight cutting edge to his voice. "But I explained all that five months ago. They never will sign as long as they can go on a de facto basis and use the fact there's no official agreement to make capital out of points like this about trading Navy equipment to aliens. Would you?''

"I suppose not,'' said Lily thoughtfully.

"I still say, ignore it—or refuse them, flat,'' said Age harshly. "What can they do about it, anyway?''

"Delay current trading sessions," said Jarl. "And they can afford to do that. We can't—I mean we here at Abruzzi Fourteen. We need that heavy machinery now. They're pinching us."

"No one ever promised them Mark," said Paul, from the end of the table.

Jarl looked down along the table at the young outposter with a hint of exasperation.

"Mark promised them Mark," Jarl said. "I thought I'd got that through all your heads. It was Mark who sent them the original agreement. Their counteroffer was on its way here —and it was a counteroffer that agreed, provided Mark would surrender himself personally to Earth justice to answer charges arising out of his actions. Then Mark took off from here—"

"Mark and Ulla," interposed Paul quietly.

"Mark and Ulla, then. What difference does Ulla make?" said Jarl. "The point is, Mark left here to give himself up to Earth. He even left a letter here for us, saying that's what he intended to do, that he anticipated Earth asking for him. Consequently, Earth claims this constituted agreement to their counterproposal, since Mark was the negotiating authority. And we can't deny he was the negotiating authority, because it's to our advantage to hold Earth to Mark's original version of the agreement. In fact, we can't deny it if we want to carry on trade and recruitment of special personnel from Earth without interruption. The only fly in the ointment is the fact Mark made some kind of shift error and got lost among the stars, before he could get to Earth."

"I suppose they really don't believe that," said Lily.

"They believe it all right," said Age. "Even if they don't, what's the difference? The ship's been lost six months. Wherever in space it is, Mark and Ulla would be dead from atmosphere exhaustion. They won't come back to bother Earth. And that's all Earth wants."

"In the large sense," said Jarl, "not the small. And it's the small I've been trying to get into your heads . . ."

Brot stiffened suddenly, squinting out the window at the recolonization cruiser. What he had been watching for had arrived. A ground car was racing up to it. Now it had halted for checking by the guarding spacemen. A young but bearded man wearing colonist clothes and a girl with the collar of her nurse's jacket turned up so that it hid her face were showing papers. Barely glancing at them, the spacemen waved them both to the fore air-lock ladder. As Brot watched, they ran for it—and made it. A moment later the lock closed and the first rumble of the cruiser's warming engines sounded.

Brot sat back in his chair, letting out the sigh of relief he had been holding, a sigh that had been waiting six months now for utterance. It was one thing to trust a woman to keep her man from throwing his life away. It was something else again to hope she could persuade him to scrap everything he had believed in while those who loved him set up an entire new life for him. Six months was a long time for a natural leader to sit it out in the mountains while his followers took over.

But the girl had done it. She had the one thing the boy lacked—an appreciation of the fact that in the end no one makes it to where he's headed entirely alone. For the second time in his life (the first had been when he had stood with Mark as a baby in his arms amid the ruins of the Ten Roos station) Brot felt a fleeting twinge of loss for the wife he had never had. But Brot was too much of a man of the immediate present to waste any emotion on might-have-beens. He turned his attention back to the meeting, to see Lily, Paul, and Maura Vols all with their eyes covertly and questioningly upon him.

He gave them a curt nod of assurance, unseen by Age or Jarl. Jarl was still talking. The other three relaxed, turning their own attention back to what the big man was saying.

"The other Colonies are voting in their own officers as fast as they can." Jarl's words seemed to float and hang in the still air of the room. "But we here at Abruzzi Fourteen are two years ahead of them, mainly because of the work I've done. And because we're ahead, we've been able to cream off the best of the available Navy ships and supplies at Navy Base for our own colony. Now, Earth can afford to take its time. The other Colonies can take their time. But we, Abruzzi Fourteen, can't afford to take *our* time, because we want to keep the natural lead we've got over the other hundred and forty-three Independent

Colonies. We're the ones who put us out ahead in the first place—"

"Were we?" Paul interrupted softly. "I thought it was Mark."

Jarl looked at him.

"As Mark himself said at the outposter meeting the day he left," answered Jarl, "he couldn't have done it without us. Oh, don't jump to the notion I'm trying to run down Mark's part in all this. If he needed us, we needed him, too. But we've got to operate without his help now, and the way to do that is to start off recognizing that it's us—all of us around this table"—his gaze swung about over them all—"who're the actual, present leaders for the Colonies, and that the Colonies lead the human race. In short, we're important people, and that means we've got a duty to our colonists—to all the colonists in general and the race as a whole—to guard that importance and take it into account in making decisions."

"You think I don't?" Age growled. "There's nobody but me to manage those factories—and there aren't any other factories, out here at least. They think I drive them too hard, those people I've got working for me. But I can afford to burn them up. I can't afford to burn *me* up."

He looked around at all the others except Jarl.

"The rest of you may not agree you're important," he said. "But I do. And that's because I am—maybe the most important."

"Not exactly," said Lily quickly. "Your factories won't be doing anything if I don't interpret the alien psychologies for all of us. Earth always had factory management, but it never had alien relations experts, and that's where the key to success lies."

"And with the trained people to handle the ships to make it all work, don't forget," said Maura. "Don't push, Age. We're all important people here. We all know it, and we're all interested in seeing our United Independent Colonies develop to everybody's best advantage—"

She looked at Jarl.

"Aren't I right, Jarl?"

"Why, yes," he said. "Self-interest—enlightened self-interest, of course—is always the best motive. That's why, with all respect to Mark"—he glanced down the table at Paul—"we're better off to have lost him. This is a new era, now, in the Colonies, and his ways belonged to the old. While we—"

Down in the landing area the recolonization cruiser finally took off with a mounting thunder of engines that momentarily drowned out all possibility of talk in the Residence library. Slowly, the sound faded, and Brot, who had turned to look out the window once more, brought his face and attention back at the library. He laughed at them all.

"There it goes," he said loudly in the new stillness, "leaving the rest of you sitting here like small frogs in a puddle, trying to blow yourselves up big in the universe. Well, you're necessary to the machinery, I guess. So if you weren't already so hell-bent to create your-

selves lords of the human race, some of the
real people would have to invent you to do the
job. But I goddam well don't have to like the
fact—or you. And I don't."

His eyes met Jarl's at the opposite end of
the long table.

"And you don't like me," Brot went on. "But
you aren't going to do anything about me.
You'll still need the outposters here for
another ten years or so—even if you like to
pretend you don't—and long before then I'll
be gone."

He pointed out the window and up in the
direction the cruiser had lifted.

"Out there," he said. "That's where the real
future is, with the people who've just left.
They've gone and left your kind sitting behind
here, talking about it. And it's out there with
them that I'm going to end up, still in the front
of the wave, with my grandchild on the one
good knee I've got left, and the bad taste of
Earth, and all of you, too, five hundred light-
years behind me."

"What're you talking about, Brot?" said
Age sourly. "Everybody knows you never had
any children. Even Mark was adopted, and
he's dead. You can move on any time you want
to, and no tears shed. But don't talk about
grandchildren to me. You'll never have anything you can even pretend to call a grandchild—any more than I ever had."

Age turned back to Jarl, opening his mouth
to take up the discussion the cruiser's lift-off
had interrupted.

"The hell I won't!" growled Brot softly, still

smiling grimly up at the skies into which the cruiser, bearing Mark and Ulla under new identities, had now flung itself out of sight, into free space and the free years to come.

Gordon R. Dickson

☐	48-537-9	Sleepwalker's World	$2.50
☐	48-580-8	The Outposter	$2.95
☐	48-525-5	Planet Run *with Keith Laumer*	$2.75
☐	48-556-5	The Pritcher Mass *February 83*	$2.75

Buy them at your local bookstore or use this handy coupon:
Clip and mail this page with your order

PINNACLE BOOKS, INC. – Reader Service Dept.
1430 Broadway, New York, NY 10018

Please send me the book(s) I have checked above. I am enclosing $_____ (please add 75¢ to cover postage and handling). Send check or money order only—no cash or C.O.D.'s.

Mr./Mrs./Miss_____

Address_____

City_____ State/Zip_____

Please allow six weeks for delivery. Prices subject to change without notice.
Canadian orders must be paid with U.S. Bank check or U.S. Postal money order only.

Best-Selling Science Fiction from TOR

☐	48-547-6	**Test of Fire** Ben Bova	$2.95
☐	48-542-5	**The Descent of Anansi** Larry Niven and Steven Barnes	$2.95
☐	48-531-X	**The Taking of Satcon Station** Barney Cohen and Jim Baen	$2.95
☐	48-555-7	**There Will Be War** J.E. Pournelle	$2.95
☐	48-512-2	**Not This August** C.M. Kornbluth revised by Frederik Pohl	$2.75
☐	48-543-3	**The Syndic** C.M. Kornbluth revised by Frederik Pohl	$2.75
☐	48-570-0	**Gunner Cade/Takeoff** C.M. Kornbluth and C.L. Moore *April 83*	$2.95

Buy them at your local bookstore or use this handy coupon:
Clip and mail this page with your order

PINNACLE BOOKS, INC. – Reader Service Dept.
1430 Broadway, New York, NY 10018

Please send me the book(s) I have checked above. I am enclosing $_____ (please add 75¢ to cover postage and handling). Send check or money order only—no cash or C.O.D.'s.

Mr./Mrs./Miss_____

Address_____

City_____ State/Zip_____

Please allow six weeks for delivery. Prices subject to change without notice.
Canadian orders must be paid with U.S. Bank check or U.S. Postal money order only.